Dear Romance Reader,

Welcome to a world of breathtaking passion and never-ending romance.
Welcome to *Precious Gem Romances.*

It is our pleasure to present *Precious Gem Romances,* a wonderful new line of romance books by some of America's best-loved authors. Let these thrilling historical and contemporary romances sweep you away to far-off times and places in stories that will dazzle your senses and melt your heart.

Sparkling with joy, laughter, and love, each *Precious Gem Romance* glows with all the passion and excitement you expect from the very best in romance. Offered at a great affordable price, these books are an irresistible value—and an essential addition to your romance collection. Tender love stories you will want to read again and again. *Precious Gem Romances* are books you will treasure forever.

Look for eight fabulous new *Precious Gem Romances* each month—available only at Wal★Mart.

Lynn Brown, Publisher

DEAR DEBORAH

Judy Christenberry

ZEBRA BOOKS
KENSINGTON PUBLISHING CORP.

ZEBRA BOOKS are published by

Kensington Publishing Corp.
850 Third Avenue
New York, NY 10022

Copyright © 1996 by Judy Christenberry

All rights reserved. No part of this book may be reproduced in any form or by any means without the prior written consent of the Publisher, excepting brief quotes used in reviews.

If you purchased this book without a cover, you should be aware that this book is stolen property. It was reported as "unsold and destroyed" to the Publisher and neither the Author nor the Publisher has received any payment for this "stripped book."

Zebra and the Z logo Reg. U.S. Pat. & TM Off.

First Printing: September, 1996
10 9 8 7 6 5 4 3 2 1

Printed in the United States of America

One

Dear Broken-hearted,
    Your difficulties touch my heart.

Deborah Townsend stared at the screen of her computer, unable to come up with another word. It was difficult to concentrate with all the turmoil going on around her.

The paper, *The Fort Worth Daily,* the city's second largest, had been sold. And with good reason. It was fading fast. The sale was good news, except that the editor, Gerald Campbell, who'd given her her first job, was retiring. Voluntarily, he said.

And the new editor was beyond belief. Movie star good looks, a background of risk-taking reporting from all over the globe, and the brother of her friend, Rachel Comisky.

Already, he was making rapid changes in the paper. Several of her old friends had moved on to other opportunities. So far, he hadn't bothered her, but she feared her time would come.

"Mrs. Townsend?"

She swung around and discovered she was right. Jason Bridges, the new editor, was lounging against the door of her cubicle, watching her. Instead of the suit and tie Mr. Campbell always wore, Bridges was dressed in khaki slacks and a knit shirt that emphasized his broad shoulders and flat stomach. She knew he had to be in his mid-thirties, but what wear and tear there was, including a tiny scar on his left cheek, only enhanced his attractiveness.

"Yes, Mr. Bridges?" She tried to hide her nervousness by folding her trembling fingers in her lap.

"There's no need to be so formal. After all, you're a friend of Rachel," he said with an easy grin. "Make it Jason."

Her mouth was full of cotton, her features rigid. She simply couldn't make herself return that smile. There was too much at stake here. Was she going to lose her job also?

"I thought we might go to lunch today, if you don't have any other commitment. Give us a chance to talk."

Deborah loved her job. She wrote a romance advice column called Heart-to-Heart for the newspaper. But she had no illusions about her importance in the scheme of things. Lunch with the editor wasn't normal.

"Why?" she abruptly asked, before blushing at her rudeness. "I mean—"

He seemed amused by her gaucheness, irritating her all the more. "I thought we'd discuss the reason over lunch."

"If you're going to—suggest I look for another position, I'd rather you just tell me. I don't need a last meal." She raised her chin several inches and tried to keep her glare steady.

Eyebrows soared to meet the thatch of dark hair that tended to fall to one side, giving him a boyish air. "Fire my sister's best friend? You must think I'm a real hatchetman, Deborah."

"Several of my friends have already left," she said stubbornly, refusing to give in to his charm.

"Are you saying I've treated people unfairly?" Some of the laziness had left his voice, and he straightened from his casual stance.

Her gaze dropped at his question. No, she couldn't say that. But she didn't like change. She didn't like losing Gerald Campbell as her editor. She didn't like—

"Deborah?" he prodded.

"No."

"Ah. Ungracious but honest." He grinned again as she looked up at him. "My kind of lady."

She knew that wasn't the truth. She felt as exciting as a dust mote next to Jason Bridges. Already, there was a concerted rush among the women in Fort Worth to make him welcome. He'd been seen several times with a stunning redhead, another friend of Rachel's.

"Lunch, Deborah?" he prodded again, but softly. "I'm starving."

She realized the man was determined, for some unknown reason. With a sigh, she said, "I'll meet you. Where shall we go?"

"Afraid to be seen leaving the building with me?" he taunted, a knowing grin on his well-shaped lips.

He didn't look much like Rachel, Deborah thought, her gaze tracing his strong features. It wasn't that he was really handsome. He was just a sexy, powerful, intelligent man who knew what he wanted and went for it. That's all. Her stomach felt queasy.

"I just thought you might have other commitments after lunch and wouldn't want to take the time to bring me back to the office," she said stiffly, knowing instinctively he could see through her excuse.

"Come on, Deborah, before I come over there and haul you out of that chair you seem to be glued to." He put his hands on his slim hips and appeared ready to do just what he'd said.

"That won't be necessary," she said in clipped tones as she picked up her purse and stood. "I was simply thinking of your convenience."

She moved to the doorway but he remained in it, staring down at her. Her throat went dry as his scent whirled around her. He seemed so much larger up close. Finally, he took her arm and started down the hallway.

"Jason, how about lunch?" one of the senior editors called out as they reached the elevator.

She peeked up at Jason's face in hope. "If you want—"

"Thanks, Tom, but I've got plans already. Maybe tomorrow."

He'd never released her arm, and the other man noted his possessive hold and suddenly grinned. "Oh, I see. Enjoy yourselves."

Deborah's cheeks flushed. In about five minutes it would be all over the paper that she was making a play for the editor. Never mind that he was the one treating her as a prisoner, cutting off the circulation in her arm. "Thanks a lot," she muttered.

"For enhancing your reputation?" he teased. "Not that I think you need it, Deborah. I'm sure your social calendar is quite full without the addition of my name." The elevator door opened and he pulled her inside.

She didn't have a social calendar, but she wasn't going to admit it to this man. "I think you can turn me loose now. I can't escape in an elevator."

"Good," he said, releasing her. "I was beginning to feel like a social outcast. You have about as much enthusiasm for lunch with me as any criminal would with a judge."

Again that easy smile, lazy, seductive, reached out to her, but she hardened her heart and took several steps away from him to lean against the wall.

"I know you're a busy man. I didn't want to take up too much of your time."

He chuckled. "You're going to have to come up with a better excuse than that, Deb, if you want me to believe you."

"The name is Deborah," she said coldly, staring at the numbers overhead as they lit up in reverse sequence.

"Are you sure you and Rachel are friends?" he questioned. Again there was a teasing note in his voice, but also a real curiosity.

Deborah could understand his confusion. Rachel was

light-hearted, teasing, completely unlike her. Once she'd been carefree and happy, too. She and Rachel had been friends at Texas Christian University. Both had married and continued their friendship. Until Randall's death.

"I haven't seen her much lately."

"And not once since I arrived have you mentioned either to me or anyone else that she's your friend. Afraid you'll be accused of pulling strings?"

Even though the elevator doors opened, Deborah stared up at him in surprise. "Being Rachel's friend wouldn't save my job if the paper is better off without me."

"You're amazing, Deborah Townsend," he said, tilting up her chin to stare at her. "Like I said, my kind of lady."

"Stop saying that! We both know it isn't true," she said, wrenching her chin from his hold.

"Well, maybe not," he agreed. "I usually prefer my women to be a little more, uh, statuesque. You look like a strong wind would blow you away."

She sent him a burning look over her shoulder as she hurried through the elevator doors before they could close.

He strolled out behind her. "This way." His hand reached for her arm again.

"I'm not going to run away, Mr. Bridges."

"I was just being friendly."

She gave up any attempt to do word battles with this man. Nothing pierced his armor. Maintaining silence, she walked beside him out of the building. They crossed the street and he held open the door to another office tower.

Frowning, she paused. "The only place to eat here is the Petroleum Club."

"Yeah. They've got great food."

She stared down at her plain denim skirt and blouse. "I'm not dressed for such a nice restaurant."

"You're fine," he assured her, his gaze lingering as it traveled up her body.

There was nothing she could object to in his words. But

the heat in his eyes stunned and confused her. Since Randall's death, she had hidden away from any man, much less one as dynamic and attractive as Jason Bridges. She rushed into the building, hoping to leave behind both his look and her awareness.

"I embarrassed you?" he asked, catching her arm to stop her rapid pace. "All I said was that you were dressed okay to eat at the Petroleum club."

"No, of course you didn't embarrass me," she muttered, lying through her teeth. How could she explain to her employer that she'd lived as a cloistered nun for the past two years and wasn't used to a man's gaze roving her body?

He released his hold on her, but his frown remained. "Okay. The elevators are over here."

"And you're hungry. I know," she said, hoping to distract him with a feeble attempt at humor. She suspected it failed miserably since her companion's frown didn't go away.

He pressed the button for the elevator. "Right." And that was the last word either spoke until they reached the restaurant.

Jason Bridges settled into the soft leather chair opposite Deborah and reached for the menu. He'd extended the invitation to her as a special favor to Rachel, his sister.

Nothing had happened as planned.

He'd figured she would play up her friendship with Rachel as a bargaining tool for keeping her job. Instead, Deborah had told no one of her connection to him. Even more surprising, she'd assured him she didn't expect to keep her job if it wasn't in the paper's best interest.

He hadn't made up his mind about that.

He only knew that when she looked up at him with those huge blue eyes, as guileless as any baby's, he'd felt like a heel for teasing her.

"Mr. Bridges—"

"Jason, Deborah. Call me Jason," he reiterated, looking up from his menu. He discovered the waitress waiting for his attention.

"Sorry. Have you ordered, Deborah?"

"Yes."

He quickly made his choices and handed the menu to the waitress, smiling in apology.

After the woman left their table, he turned his attention to Deborah, who sat staring out the window. She wasn't anything like he'd pictured. In spite of her thinness, she had curves that would distract any man. In fact, if she didn't make such a concerted effort to appear sexless, drawing her blond hair back into a tight knot, wearing loose fitting clothing and no make-up, she'd be a knock-out.

"Deborah," he began but paused when she turned those wide blue eyes, filled with apprehension, on him.

"Quit looking like I'm about to toss you out the window. You make me feel like a monster," he complained with a smile.

Her lashes quickly veiled her gaze from him and she reached for her glass of water. "Sorry. I guess I'm just a little concerned about the reason for our lunch meeting."

With a shrug of his shoulders, he confessed, "I offered lunch because of Rachel. She asked me to—" he broke off, unsure how to phrase Rachel's request. She'd asked him to take care of her friend, treat her gently, protect her.

"What?"

"Make an effort to get to know you," he substituted. "She assures me you're a top notch writer."

"I don't need special treatment, Mr. Br—Jason. There are better writers. I enjoy what I do, but I know the reality of the newspaper world."

"Which is?"

"If it doesn't sell papers, it won't be retained."

"And does your column sell papers?"

He watched her throw back her shoulders and lift her

chin. He liked her spirit, even though it always surprised him. There was more to her than beauty and softness.

"I like to think so. I receive about thirty letters a week asking for advice."

Rubbing his chin, he waited. Silence was sometimes the best response.

"I know that's not a lot, but it matters to those people," she assured him earnestly.

"Do any of them ever write you back, tell you how your advice worked?"

Lashes dropped to hide her eyes, drawing his interest.

"Yes, sometimes."

Before he could pursue that train of thought, the waitress interrupted them with their meal.

While pretending to concentrate on the steak he was cutting, Jason watched his companion pick at her food. The only sign of vanity were her nails, polished a soft pink. Intrigued by the contrast of painted nails to no-lipstick lips, he wondered why she downplayed her femininity.

She looked up, catching his eyes on her, and hurriedly turned away. "Do you intend to keep the column?"

Her directness surprised him. "Of course, in some form or other. I have a few ideas for changing it, though. Are you an adaptable person?"

Her shoulders stiffened and she met his gaze head on. "Maybe. What kind of changes?"

He grinned. If he touched on personal matters, she ran away, but if he talked about the professional side of her life, she faced him without hesitation. Interesting.

"Well, for one thing, I think you need to lighten up."

"I beg your pardon?" she responded with a look of astonishment.

"Where's your sense of humor? Your advice is okay, though a little out-dated, but it's too intense."

"The people who write me are hurting. Their problems are very serious to them. You think I should laugh at them?"

He could tell by her rising voice that she was outraged. She lowered her fork to the table and sat back in her chair, frowning fiercely.

"Laugh with them, not at them." Before he could expound on his words, she pounced.

"A broken heart isn't funny. Probably you've never experienced such a thing, but it's not a laughing matter."

"And just how many broken hearts have *you* experienced?" he demanded in return, glad to have pierced her reserve.

A look of pain shot through her expression and she picked up her fork again. "Just one," she muttered, concentrating on her dinner.

Damn. He'd forgotten. Rachel had warned him about Deborah's husband's death. With her virginal appearance, he hadn't linked Deborah with any man.

Feeling like a bully, he hastily apologized. "I'm sorry. Rachel told me—"

Her head came up swiftly and she glared at him. "I don't require special treatment," she whispered fiercely. "If you're going to fire me, just get on with it."

"Would you quit suggesting that I'm going to fire you? You're the only one who's mentioned firing. I'm beginning to think that's what you want."

"Don't be silly!" she snapped. "I love my job."

"And I think your column is important to the future of the paper," he said firmly and was rewarded by the easing of her stiff shoulders. When she finally looked at him, he added, "I just think it could be improved."

As if preparing herself for a blow, she lowered her fork to the table again and leaned back in her chair. "How?"

He tried a different tack. "Tell me about your personal life."

She ran away again. "My personal life has nothing to do with my work."

"I think it does."

She struggled to control her anger. He watched her efforts reflected in her delicate features. She really was a beauty. It was a good thing blondes weren't his type. They always seemed too delicate, too . . . too soft. He liked strong women.

"You've already said I give sound advice. That's all that matters in an advice column." Her words, as well as her expression, were cold and closed.

"When's the last time you went out on a date?" he asked, taking a stab in the dark.

She looked out the window and he wasn't sure she would answer him. Finally, she turned and stared at him, a challenge in her eyes. "Eight years ago."

"Eight years? What were you, a child?" he demanded incredulously. Her flawless complexion made her look about eighteen.

"I'm the same age as Rachel, twenty-eight, and you know it," she snapped. "Just what kind of a game are you playing? My personal life has nothing to do with my work."

"You're wrong. How can you give advice on dating when you don't even know what's going on out there?'

"Matters of the heart haven't changed. That's why Shakespeare is still so popular. He understood people's emotions. Are you going to tell me *he's* outdated?" she challenged.

"No, but I doubt I'd hire him to write an advice column," Jason returned. "Did you ever face the issue of condoms when you were dating?"

Her eyes widened and she hurriedly looked around as if afraid someone would overhear them. "I really don't think such a discussion is necessary."

"Why not? That's what women are facing these days. At least I hope they are. And what about date rape? Or con men? Don't you get letters about those things?"

"Yes, I do, and I don't have to experience date rape to know how to respond," she assured him intensely.

"I didn't mean to imply that. But I didn't see any letters

touching those subjects in recent columns. All you wrote
about was love and broken hearts and lots of talk about
forgiveness." He leaned forward. "Are you telling me you
get letters about those subjects, but you never print them?"

"I choose which letters to print by what I think my readers want to hear. I want my column to be uplifting, full of
hope and encouragement." She was returning to that prim,
virginal void rather than the fiery combatant he'd just faced.

"*I* think your readers want to hear the truth."

"How dare you? I always print the truth! I never change
the letters."

"That's not what I meant," he assured her. "I think you're
not printing the truth about the dating scene. That's what
your column is all about, isn't it, Deborah? Men and women
who are dating, trying to find that certain someone to love?"

"Of course it is. Do you really think a discussion of condoms is going to encourage them, make them believe love
is possible?" She glared at him. "Or maybe you'd prefer a
discussion of various sexually transmitted diseases? We
could feature a disease a week. Wouldn't that be charming?"

He'd certainly roused her fighting side again. Her eyes
flashed and strands of blond hair popped loose from the
tight knot as if they had a life of their own.

"That's not exactly what I had in mind, but there *will* be
changes in your column, Deborah Townsend, whether you
like it or not."

"Then maybe I'd better do your job for you and fire myself
before we go any further!" She threw her napkin across her
almost full plate, picked up her purse, stood and walked out.

So much for treating Deborah Townsend with kid gloves.
Rachel was going to kill him.

Two

Deborah was angry. With herself. She didn't want to leave her job. But she'd opened her mouth and inserted both feet.

"Nice move, Deborah, really nice move," she muttered as she crossed the street to the newspaper's office. The man hadn't fired her. She'd fired herself.

She jabbed the button for the elevator. Depression was replacing her anger. For two years, writing her column had been her life. What would she have once her work was gone?

As she entered her office, a small voice in the far reaches of her mind whispered, *You could apologize.*

"A lot of good that would do me. He doesn't like my work," she said aloud, sinking into her chair. A new stack of letters waiting on the desk caught her eye. She picked up several of the envelopes. Just holding them filled her with warmth, a sense of purpose. Her eyes lit up when she recognized a return address. Manny! She started to rip open the envelope and then stopped.

She wasn't the author of Heart-to-Heart anymore. A new surge of despair rolled over her. Then her lips firmed and she finished opening Manny's letter. *This* letter was to *her,* not the columnist.

Dear Deborah,
　　I followed your advice and Elizabeth loved the evening. I tried to do just as you said. Now I have another

problem. I want to ask Elizabeth to marry me. Can you help me figure out what to say? I'll be waiting for your answer.

Manny

Deborah smiled. Manny was ready to propose to Elizabeth. She sighed with delight.

"Not angry anymore?" Jason's baritone shattered her pleasure.

Immediately, her smile disappeared and she stiffened her spine. "Of course not, Mr. Bridges."

Without waiting for an invitation, he stepped into her cubicle and sat in the chair across from her desk. He put a styrofoam carton in front of her.

"What's that?" she demanded.

"Your dinner. I paid for it, so you might as well have it to eat later, when you're not angry. By the way, I thought redheads were supposed to have tempers, not blondes."

Visions of Mariana, the redhead rumored to be Jason's love interest, flashed into Deborah's head. She avoided his gaze. "I don't have a temper."

He grinned. "Could've fooled me."

As if to contradict herself, her temper flared again, but she quickly reined it in. "If you'll excuse me, I need to pack my things." She opened a drawer and pretended to organize her belongings. Surreptitiously she peeped at her visitor to see if he took the hint to leave.

"Come on, Deborah. I didn't take your resignation seriously."

Deborah's teeth sank into her bottom lip. Here was her opportunity. She fingered Manny's letter. Finally, she raised her gaze to Jason's. She saw a glint of humor as well as understanding in his eyes. "I suppose I did lose my temper."

"Whew! That's a relief. I was afraid you were going to stonewall me," he admitted, his lips spreading into a warm grin.

Deborah blinked several times. The man's charm was potent. She sat up a little straighter and tried to concentrate on what was important, her job. "I realize you will probably bring in someone else, but—"

"Wait a minute. There you go putting words into my mouth again. Why would I do that?"

He leaned toward her and her office space suddenly seemed to evaporate. She pressed back against her chair. "You said there had to be changes," she reminded him breathlessly.

"So? Are you telling me you're totally inflexible?"

"No," she said slowly, trying to work her way through his meaning. "But you don't like my writing."

"I never said that." After pausing, he added, "In fact, I found your writing charming . . . if you were sixty years old."

Her palms smacked down on her desk and she leaned forward. "I do not write like an old lady! Just because I don't discuss certain subjects in my column does not mean that my advice is irrelevant and unimportant!"

He raised both hands in mock surrender. "Let's not start World War III. I think if we work together, we can come up with a compromise."

Deborah frowned. She didn't like the sound of his suggestion. "Surely you don't intend to personally supervise my column? Louise has always looked it over before we go to press."

He studied her with those hazel eyes that seemed to see right through her. "Why does the idea of working with me bother you? I'm going to get a complex."

"No, I didn't mean to sound—I know how important your job is and how much you have to do. I just don't want to overburden you. If you'll tell me how you want the column to change, I'll do the best I can."

Running a hand through his dark hair, he continued to

study her. "Hmmm. Well, we could try that, if I saw some signs that you're making changes."

"Of course," she eagerly agreed. She didn't want close supervision by the man across from her. In fact, for her peace of mind, she'd be happy to never see him again. His overtly masculine presence toppled the safe little world she'd built around her the past two years.

"I don't want to overwhelm you," he said consideringly. "How about if I give you one change at a time? If you successfully complete that change, then we move on to the next."

"That sounds quite reasonable . . . Jason," she added to show her desire to cooperate. She'd never called her previous editor anything other than Mr. Campbell, but if Jason Bridges wanted everything informal, she'd be informal. Small price to pay for him to leave her alone.

"You're attending the reception for Campbell tomorrow evening?"

She frowned in confusion. What happened to the changes he wanted made? "Yes, of course."

"Good. I want to see a different you."

"I beg your pardon?" she gasped, stunned and confused. How had they gone from discussing changes in her column to her social calendar?

"Show me you can enter the nineties. That's the first step to changing your column."

"Mr. Bridges! My personal life is none of your business! I agreed to make changes in my column, not in my life. I don't even know what you mean, but I have no intention of changing myself!"

"Then I don't think you can write the column."

Pain pierced her heart. He couldn't take her job away from her. She needed it! Before she could decide whether to grovel at his feet and plead, he spoke again.

"Come on, Deborah, don't be so difficult. All I'm talking about is a nice dress, casual social interaction. Don't tell

me you've always dressed like this?" He gestured toward
her jean skirt and blouse.

She wanted to fling his insulting remark back in his face.
She was perfectly presentable! Fear of losing her job and
just a smidgin of self-honesty made her hesitate.

She gnawed on her bottom lip. Since Randall's death,
she'd dressed as she was now. Life had been too painful to
interact with other people. She'd wanted to hide, and she'd
done so with her appearance. Admitting such behavior to
herself was one thing. Admitting it to the man across from
her was another.

"My appearance has nothing to do with my writing."

"You're wrong. A good journalist must get involved in
life, must be able to understand his readers' point of view.
I want your column to attract a lot of attention. I want to
syndicate it. If I can do that, our paper could become syn-
onymous with your column throughout America, just like
the Chicago papers are for Ann Landers and Siskel &
Ebert."

His voice was full of enthusiasm, moving Deborah away
from the personal aspects of his words. To be syndicated
was a lofty ambition, one she'd harbored in the fartherest
regions of her mind.

"Try it, Deborah," he whispered, drawing her gaze back
to him. "Try just this one little step. Then we'll talk again."

"That's all I have to do? Dress up for Mr. Campbell's
party?"

"That's all for the moment. Oh, and look for letters that
are a little more controversial than a first kiss."

She frowned. He'd slid the selection of her letters in at
the last minute as if it wasn't important. He was a master
strategist. "Are you asking me to submit them to you for
approval?"

"No. I'm asking you to consider the entertainment value
of your column beyond just the one reader whose problem
you're solving. That's all."

She could agree. Or she could quit. Having come so close to losing her job twice already, she couldn't take the second option. Would it be so bad to dress up, maybe wear make-up? Couldn't she select more exciting letters? She'd responded to several, but she'd never printed them.

Finally, she raised her gaze to her new editor. "All right," she agreed with a reluctant sigh, "I'll try, but I'm not promising sensationalism."

"Great. If you need help, call Rachel."

"Call Rachel to choose the letters I put in the column?" she demanded incredulously. He was carrying this family thing a little far.

He chuckled. "No, Deborah. I meant about the dress and, uh, makeup or whatever. I'll trust your judgment on the letters. Rachel would go for sensationalism in a minute."

In one fluid movement, he rose and strode from her office with a wave of his hand in goodbye. Deborah sat in stunned silence. Her comfortable world had been turned upside down in less than an hour.

Damn! What had he gotten himself into? One minute he was trying to improve the column, the next he was on a one man rescue mission. He hadn't been so taken in by sad eyes since he was eight years old and lost his heart to a puppy in the pet store. Not that he intended to lose his heart to Deborah Townsend, though she had a lot more to offer than a puppy.

The woman Rachel had described, had talked about through the years, wasn't anything like the Deborah Townsend he took to lunch. Somehow, he'd never met Rachel's good friend, though they'd both been in attendance at the wedding. He'd had to catch a plane immediately after the ceremony. But Rachel had always talked about Deborah.

He remembered stories of Deborah doing outrageous things in college, of her shocking the very conservative family into which she'd married, and her cheering Rachel up when she lost her baby. For that alone, he owed Deborah Townsend the world.

Rachel was his only sister, his baby sister. When he'd heard that she was expecting, he was thrilled. He didn't intend to settle down, raise a family, and he saw himself living vicariously through Rachel and her children. He'd been in Africa when his mother reached him to tell him Rachel had lost her baby.

The letter he'd finally received from Rachel mentioned Deb over and over again. He'd made a mental note then that he would someday show his gratitude to Deborah Townsend.

Today he'd sat across from a pale ghost of the woman he'd imagined. He'd seen the pain in her eyes even as she walked away from a job she obviously loved. And he couldn't let her go. Not like that. He owed her.

He strode into his office without even acknowledging his secretary's greeting. Reaching for the phone as he sat down, he punched the fast dial button that would give him Rachel.

"Hello?"

"You've gotten me in a mess, little sister."

"Jason! What are you talking about?"

"I took your dear friend, Deborah, to lunch."

"And?"

He ran a hand through his hair. How could he explain what had happened? Now he wished he hadn't called.

When he didn't respond right away, she asked, "What happened? Did you like her? She's terrific, but, well, maybe you wouldn't see that. She's—"

"Will you let me get a word in edgewise?" he demanded in exasperation. Rachel had been a talker from the crib. He'd been so proud of her first word, not realizing she'd scarcely draw breath for the next twenty-seven years.

"You weren't saying anything. Oh, Jase, don't tell me you didn't like her?" she cried out suddenly.

"I didn't say that! I don't know why I called you, brat."

" 'Cause you love me," she teased. "Come on, tell me what happened."

"I'm trying. It's just—she may call you about makeup and stuff."

Dead silence, a surprise anytime it happened with Rachel. Finally, she said, "What are you talking about?"

"I, uh, I told her she had to dress up for the party tomorrow night. Are you and Paul coming?"

"Yes. What are you talking about makeup? Doesn't she wear any now?"

"Doesn't look like it to me, but I'm no expert. She's as pale as a ghost. And she dresses like a nun."

"Deb?" Rachel asked incredulously.

"Haven't you seen her lately?"

"No," his sister said slowly. "I haven't seen her in over a year. She was dressed rather drably then, but I thought she'd have gotten over it by now. Every time I've called and asked her to lunch or dinner, she's had an excuse. I thought she didn't want to be around me and Paul because we're together while she's alone."

"Well, hopefully you'll see her tomorrow night. If she calls you for help, don't ask any questions, okay?"

"Jason, Deb doesn't need any help with makeup or clothes. *She* taught *me!*"

"Damn! I'm glad to know who to blame for the way you look," he teased. "Gotta go."

He hung up to her amused outrage, a typical reaction to his teasing.

"You busy now, Jason?" Tom Langford, the editor he'd seen earlier at the elevator, popped his head in the door.

"No, Tom, come on in."

"I wanted to be sure I wasn't interrupting anything, like a long lunch," the man hinted, waggling his eyebrows.

Jason rolled his eyes in response. "Business, Tom, just business. I need to revamp a few things."

"Well, Deborah's not a bad place to start. But you'll probably get frost-bite. That's what happens to anyone who's gotten close to her lately."

"Don't worry about me. The lady's not my type. Now, what did you need to see me about?"

Deborah studied her dress in front of the mirror. After a going-over of her wardrobe the night before, she'd realized nothing fit properly. The weight she'd dropped after Randall's death made the clothes she'd worn before hang on her. All she'd bought the past two years were casual, nondescript clothes.

Since Randall came from an old Fort Worth family, its money in oil and farmland, they'd made the social rounds until he grew ill. After his death, she'd refused all invitations.

Well, she wasn't going to let Jason Bridges think she didn't know how to dress. With all the fortitude of a martyr, she'd left work early this afternoon and marched two streets over to an expensive dress shop she'd frequented in the past.

Now she chuckled aloud at herself, something she hadn't done in a while. How self-righteous she'd felt until she realized she was having fun.

"Oh , Mrs. Townsend, with the weight you lost, this dress would be stunning," the saleslady had assured her, holding up the dress she was now wearing.

Though it was black, there was nothing quiet about it. The vee neck, low enough to show her curves, was outlined in black sequins, just to draw attention to those curves. The back was nonexistent. Thank goodness it had a built-in bra.

She examined her profile, wondering if she'd gotten carried away with showing Jason Bridges. It was certainly a daring dress. But if Mariana was accompanying Jason, he'd never notice *her.*

Shoving aside such thoughts, assuring herself she didn't

want Jason's attention, only his approval of her column, she set about showing him she also knew how to use make-up to her advantage.

An hour later, she entered the hotel ballroom the city fathers had set aside for honoring a man who had served his city well. She greeted Gerald Campbell, accepting his surprised compliments, before moving into the room. Having arrived alone, she looked for familiar faces.

"Deb!"

She turned, recognizing Rachel's voice at once. The beautiful brunette was waving at her from across the room. She joined her and her husband, Paul.

"How nice to see you, Rachel," she said, hugging her old friend.

"Nice to see me? After avoiding me for more than a year, that's all you can say?" Rachel said as she stepped back. "Oh, Deb, you look terrific!" She turned to her husband who stepped forward to hug Deborah. "Doesn't she, Paul?"

"How should I answer that, Deb? If I agree with her, she'll get jealous. If I don't, she'll get mad."

"Just tell her I'm the second best-looking woman here," Deb offered with a grin.

"Sharp as a tack, as usual," he said. "We've missed you. How have you been?"

His quiet sincerity tugged at her emotions even more then Rachel's exuberance. Blinking rapidly to dispel the moisture that gathered in her eyes, she said, "I've missed both of you, too, but—I couldn't—"

"Oh, honey, we understood," Rachel quickly assured her, hugging her again. She pulled away and frowned at Deborah. "Turn around."

"What?" Deborah asked, puzzled.

"Turn around. I want to see the back of that dress."

Deborah grinned at Rachel's stern, schoolteacher voice. With a demure smile, she spun around. When she came back to face her friend, her smile widened. "Do you like it?"

"I don't know about Rachel, but I do," Paul said, leering at her.

"Oh, you!" Rachel protested, slapping him on the arm. "Yes, I like it, but I'm shocked, of course."

"Don't give me that," Deborah protested. "This dress has twice as much material as that purple thing you wore to Paul's fraternity party when you wanted him to propose."

"And it worked, too," Rachel crowed, leaning into her husband's adoring embrace.

"Shoot, Rachel, I was going to propose no matter what you wore. You know that."

Deborah looked away. Their happiness was wonderful, but it was like giving a woman dying of thirst a teaspoonful of water. All it did was make her thirstier. Their happiness made Deborah's loneliness all the more painful.

As if recognizing her discomfort, Rachel turned the attention back to her friend. "So, who are you trying to lure into your web, Madam Spider?"

"No one!" Deborah hastily assured her. "No one at all."

Jason escorted Mariana through the receiving line, trying to hide his irritation. He'd wanted to be here early, to watch for Deborah's arrival. Instead, he'd sat in Mariana's living room, chatting with her parents, while she primped upstairs. What was she doing still living at home anyway? he thought in irritation.

He shook hands in a distracted fashion, his eyes searching the crowd, particularly the corners, for a quiet blonde, hiding away from everyone.

Damn, maybe she hadn't come. But she'd promised. He was curious to see how she'd respond to his request. Maybe he should say order. There'd be hell to pay in the morning if she didn't show up.

"Why are you acting like a grizzly bear, honey!" Mariana drawled, batting her fake lashes.

She was a beautiful woman, but he was growing weary of her southern belle act. Fort Worth wasn't exactly South Carolina. "I'm not acting like a bear. I just wanted to be on time."

She pushed her full bottom lip forward in a practiced pout. "I said I was sorry. But it takes time to look like this." She spread her arms wide and waited for a compliment.

He ran his gaze up her red sequined dress, molded to her spectacular figure. No subtlety there. "Yes, I'm sure it does," he murmured, his gaze returning to the crowd.

"Well, I declare! Sometimes I just don't think you're worth the effort, Jason."

"And you're probably right. Come on, let's look for Rachel and Paul." He pulled her along behind him, ignoring her protests. Rachel would know if Deborah had arrived and was hiding out behind a plant somewhere in typical Cinderella fashion.

He spotted Paul's tall figure across the room. There were a number of people grouped around him. As Jason got closer, he realized it wasn't Paul, or Rachel, who was drawing the crowd, but a stunning blonde. At least what he could see was stunning. Her dress bared a creamy back that made him long to run his fingers down it. The dress itself clung in all the right places.

Snapping his attention back to the matter at hand, finding Deborah, he focused on his sister. Reaching the group, he nodded at Paul but spoke to Rachel.

"Sis, have you see Deborah yet?"

The sexy blonde turned to smile at him.

"Why, hello, Jason. How nice to see you."

Three

Jason swallowed, his mouth dry, and hoped he hid his astonishment. Deborah was the sexy blonde? He cast a quick glance at her back just to be sure she was one and the same woman. Paul sent him a knowing grin that brought heat to his cheeks.

"Jason?" Mariana demanded. "Aren't you going to introduce me?"

Grateful for the distraction, he introduced his date to the men standing around Deborah. When he brought his gaze back to Deborah, he noticed the front of her dress for the first time. He looked up to see a challenge in her eyes.

"Nice dress," he murmured with an air of casual dismissal. At least he hoped he was able to carry it off. His heart was thumping like a drum and other parts of his body were responding as well.

"Then I meet your standards?" she prodded with a superior smile.

Damn. She knew she looked terrific. Not in the self-satisfied way Mariana asked for compliments but as if she were winning points in a competition. And he'd vote for her hands down.

He'd always been a good loser. Leaning over, he whispered in her ear, "You bet. You're absolutely stunning."

She surprised him by blushing and looking away. The

man beside her, Richard Estes, took advantage of her turning in his direction and engaged her in conversation.

Richard was a local banker Jason had met when he first came to town. He watched for his opportunity and inserted himself into the conversation.

"Did you like that movie?" he asked Richard when he mentioned a film that just came out. "I haven't seen it yet."

"It's not bad. The one I'm waiting for is the adventure film with Harrison Ford. It's due out next week," Richard enthused. "Do you like the movies?" he asked Deborah.

"Yes, but I haven't seen any recent films."

"How about going to see the Ford movie next week with me? I'll take you to dinner afterwards," Richard suggested, his gaze fastened hopefully on Deborah.

Jason know she was going to refuse. He could see it in her face. To forestall her, he said, "That's a great idea. May Mariana and I join you, make it a foursome?"

"I don't think—" Deborah began, the warmth fleeing her expression. She actually took a step back from the two men.

Richard seemed to realize his only chance was to join forces with Jason. "How about it, Deborah? You're not going to turn down your boss, are you? I'll pick everyone up. I just got a new Cadillac. There's plenty of room. Do you like La Belle Vue, that new French restaurant? We could have a late meal after the movie. I'll check the times and call everyone."

Again Deborah tried to protest when the man finally drew breath, but Jason pressed her arm and spoke over her soft voice "Sounds great, Richard. Oh, I think Mrs. Carson is trying to get your attention."

The grand dame of Fort Worth society was indeed waving in their direction, and Richard nodded and hurried across the room.

"I don't intend to go to the movies with Richard," Deborah said firmly, her chin rising stubbornly.

The desire to kiss her until she was soft and pliant in his

arms, all stubbornness forgotten, surprised him. He dropped her arm as if he'd been burnt. "I think you should."

"What you think doesn't matter."

"Have you forgotten I'm your employer?" He hoped *he* hadn't.

He regretted his words as soon as he said them. He'd never tried to strongarm anyone, much less a woman. "I'm sorry, Deborah," he said, as she glared at him. "I didn't mean to imply I'd force you. But I think you need to reconsider—"

"Jason," Mariana interrupted, sliding her hand under his arm. "What are you two talking about?" Her gaze whipped back and forth between the two of them.

"We're discussing going to the movies with Deborah and Richard next weekend and then having dinner at a French restaurant," Jason said smoothly, his gaze never leaving Deborah's face.

"Ooh! I love French food. Just as long as the movie isn't something gruesome, I'm ready."

"It's the new Harrison Ford movie." He continued to stare at Deborah.

"Terrific! I love to watch him, almost as much as I love to watch you, Jason, darling," Mariana drawled, pressing against him.

Deborah looked at the other woman and then at him again. "I don't know if I'll be able to make it."

"If Richard needs a date, I have several friends who'd be glad to go out with him," Mariana suggested. Jason noted a triumphant expression on her face that irritated him.

"We'll discuss this tomorrow, at work," he assured Deborah, trying to convey with his tone that she shouldn't turn down the invitation until she talked with him.

Deborah sat at her desk, the day's letters before her, staring into space. Last night had been a mistake. She'd gotten carried away with proving to Jason Bridges that she could dress as well as the next woman. She'd overdone it. But she grudgingly admitted that it had felt good.

Tho thought that she would enjoy another man's admiration left her stunned. For two years she'd told herself she would never have an interest in any man, ever again. She felt uneasy about the discovery that she was still human.

Shaking her head, she tried to concentrate on the letters. They had always taken her away from her own troubles. But the jangle of the gold earrings she'd put on this morning only reminded her of the changes she'd made in her appearance. Gone was the baggy, sexless clothing. Today she wore grey slacks that, while not tight, didn't hide her femininity, topped with a pale pink silk blouse.

"We need to talk, Deborah," Jason Bridges announced as he strolled into her cubicle.

She told herself the leap of her heart was because of the suddenness of his arrival.

"What about?"

"You know what about. Richard just called me. It seems you went right home and called and refused the invitation he'd extended."

"Yes, it seems I did."

"Did you do it just to annoy me?" He glowered at her, his hazel eyes boring into her.

She could feel awareness coursing through her veins and willed it to stop. "Of course not. I called Richard because I don't intend to go. It only seemed fair to let him know."

"And you know I wanted you to wait until we had discussed the idea."

"Since you're not my father," Deborah said, "I couldn't see any reason to discuss my *personal* life with you."

"My point exactly."

Staring at him blankly, she said, "I don't understand what you mean."

"I mean we're discussing your work, not your personal life."

"My work has nothing to do with going out with Richard."

"Yes, it does. Look, I'll concede that you know how to attract men. In fact, I'll give you a glowing recommendation in seductive dressing."

"I didn't intend—I just wanted to prove a point," she protested. "I didn't set out to seduce anyone." *Certainly not Richard,* the unbidden thought popped into her head. Her cheeks flamed and she hoped he couldn't read her mind.

"The poor guy never knew what hit him," Jason muttered wryly, a sideways grin on his face.

"This is a ridiculous conversation. I need to write my column." She shifted some letters, as if she were organizing them, hoping he'd take the hint and leave. She was still feeling rather warm and uncomfortable. Her comfort zone that she'd worked so hard to establish the past two years was quickly eroding and it was all this man's fault.

"Your work is the point I'm trying to get to," he insisted, leaning toward her.

"I've thought about what you said," she hurriedly inserted, hoping to forestall any more conversation. "I'm trying to be sure I include a variety of letters."

"That's good, but I'm still not convinced you can offer up-to-date advice. After all, you haven't been on the dating scene in a long time."

"I told you—"

"I know what you told me. Human relationships don't change. Look at Shakespeare. But Shakespeare would be laughed out of the place if he turned up looking like he did."

"I'm not likely to recommend someone wear a doublet and tights when he goes on a date," she replied drily.

"No, you've proven you've got the dress thing down pat," he assured her, his gaze roving her trim figure, noting the jewelry, her hair in a looser, more flattering style. "In fact, you look almost as good today as you did last night. I'm surprised any of the men around you can even concentrate."

His sudden compliment left her speechless, her cheeks flaming. She pulled herself together to protest, "You're being ridiculous."

"If you think that, you don't know anything about the way a man thinks."

"I really do have to get to work," she muttered, dropping her gaze to her desk. The man was making her crazy.

"I'm not leaving until we finish this thing."

"What thing?" she asked, having lost track of the point of their conversation, if it had a point.

"Your going out with Richard Estes."

"Jason, that's my *personal* business. It has nothing to do with you," she protested again.

"And that's my point. You may know how to *look* the part of a modern young women on the dating scene. I don't believe you can *act* the part." He leaned back in his chair, his arms crossed over his broad chest, and waited, a superior look on his face.

Frustrated, she studied his strong features and saw no softness. He wasn't going to give in. She knew he couldn't force her to go out with Richard. But she wanted to keep her job. And if Jason didn't believe her capable of offering advice to others, he had every right to dismiss her.

"Jason—"

He held up a hand. "All I'm asking is that you go to the movies and dinner with the man. You don't even have to kiss him goodnight."

Her eyes widened at the mere thought of allowing Richard Estes to touch her in such a personal manner. "This is crazy," she protested. Her hands were clenched on her desk.

Jason reached over and placed his big hand over the two of hers. The warmth traveled right up her arms. She looked into his hazel eyes and felt as if a chasm had ruptured in her defenses. Jason Bridges was a potent, sexy man.

"In fact, I'd prefer that you didn't kiss him goodnight. I'm not sure I like Richard all that much."

"Whether or not I kiss a man has nothing to do with your opinion of him!"

"Okay, kiss him if you want. It's up to you."

"I didn't say—" She broke off in exasperation. "What do I have to agree to so that you'll leave my office?"

"To go out with Richard, Mariana and me on Friday night to the movies and dinner. And to show a little more variety is your letter choice, and to lighten up some with your answers."

"Is that all?" she demanded sarcastically. "Are you sure you don't want me to advertise in the Personals column, or hang out at a singles bar?"

"Now that you mention it," he began with a big grin.

"Forget it! I'll go to the movies and dinner, but that's the only concession I'll make to your ridiculous doubts. After Friday night, I don't want to hear another word about my personal life. We're going to keep our conversations strictly business!"

An innocent look sat ridiculously on his strong features. "Why, of course, Deborah. That's all our conversations have ever been."

Deborah glared at him. "I don't know why you haven't been murdered in your sleep long before now."

"Because I'm much too loveable," he teased. He stood and moved to the door. "Don't worry. You won't have to put up with me for too long. I'll only be around for about six months, and then you'll be left in peace."

He strolled from her office, leaving Deborah staring at the empty doorway.

What had she done? For two years, she'd refused to reach out to anyone, filled with the pain of losing someone. Now, the first time she emerges from her protective shell, she is attracted to a handsome face who has promised to go away.

Stunned by the admission that she had any interest in Jason Bridges, Deborah could only shake her head and swallow the tears that threatened to fall. She *couldn't* have any feelings for the man. She just couldn't.

But she'd known it all along, a little voice whispered. Why else had she dressed like that last night? It wasn't for Richard Estes, or any other man. She'd dressed for Jason Bridges.

She scarcely knew him. Probably what she was experiencing was infatuation, nothing more. And it would be reasonable that she felt something for him. Hadn't Rachel talked endlessly about him? She'd heard tales of Jason and his exploits, his daring, his courage, for years. She'd also heard the love in Rachel's voice for her only brother.

Somehow she wasn't reassured. What a ridiculous turn of events.

In spite of telling herself she was crazy to even concern herself with Jason Bridges, she picked up the phone and dialed Rachel's number.

After several minutes of chatting about the previous evening and how nice it had been to see each other, Deborah eased into the real reason for her call.

"Jason and I were just discussing my column."

"Oh? I hope he appreciates you," Rachel returned.

"Well, he has some ideas for changes, but I don't think they'll be a problem. I'd kind of gotten into a rut."

"You didn't look like it last night. Paul mentioned that dress at breakfast this morning."

"I'll tell you where I bought it. They have a couple of dresses that made that one look old-maidish. The only thing Paul wouldn't like would be the bill."

Rachel giggled. "You've got a deal."

"By the way," Deborah said, hoping she sounded off-hand. "Jason mentioned he'd only be here about six months.

He left before I could ask him what he meant. Isn't he the permanent Editor-in-chief?"

"No. He just promised Dad he'd try to shape things up and find a good editor before he left." Rachel sighed. "He wants to go back to his old job of foreign correspondent. He says life in Fort Worth is just too dull for him."

"Oh."

"Mom and Dad are secretly hoping he'll change his mind, but I doubt it. If you can persuade him to stay, though, I'll be on your side. I miss him."

"I was just curious," Deborah hurriedly said. "His leaving has nothing to do with me. Maybe Mariana will entice him to stay."

"Somehow I don't think so. She called me this morning to complain. It seems Jason doesn't appreciate her," Rachel said drily.

Deborah clamped down immediately on the relief that filled her. "She's very attractive."

"She's as hot as they come," Rachel corrected. "But Jason's not interested. She tried to seduce him last night and he ignored her."

"You mean they're not—I mean, I just assumed—" Deborah was embarrassed at her prying, but she couldn't resist.

"Apparently not, or Mariana wouldn't be complaining, now, would she?"

Deborah pictured Jason in her mind's eye and agreed with Rachel. No woman would complain if Jason was her lover. The very thought of going to bed with him stirred a hunger that surprised Deborah with its intensity. "Um, I guess not."

She rapidly brought their conversation to a close. Much longer and Rachel might discover how much her brother had upset Deborah. Not that he intended to. At least, not in the way he had.

She was infatuated with him. She refused to believe it could be anything but a passing fancy.

What was she going to do now?

* * *

Jason strode from Deborah's office with a smile on his face. Mission accomplished. He'd convinced Deborah she needed to go out with Richard Estes to prove to him she could handle dating.

By the time he reached the elevator, his grin had disappeared, replaced by a heavy frown. He hoped Richard appreciated what he'd done for him.

He called the man to tell him the date was confirmed. Earlier, he'd tried to explain Deborah's reluctance to Richard. Now he emphasized his point again.

"Deborah hasn't dated since her husband's death, Richard. Just keep everything casual Friday evening. Okay?"

"Sure, Jason. It'll just be a group of friends out for the evening."

"You'd better pick me up first, just to emphasize that point to Deborah."

"I really think you're getting carried away, Bridges," Richard said stiffly. "I don't need your supervision."

"Better pick me up first or the date's off."

"I'll just call Deborah on my own," Richard assured him.

"You can try. The only reason she's going is because I told her it wasn't a date. One on one, she's not going to go." He only hoped he was right. If she agreed to accompany Richard without him and Mariana, he'd look like a fool.

"If she's that reluctant to be with me, perhaps I should—"

Damn. Now he'd overdone it. "It's not that, Richard. I thought I explained. She's just afraid to try dating again since Randall's death. Surely you can understand that?"

"Well, of course, I can, but I certainly don't want to force myself on her."

"You're not." *I am.* He shoved that thought away. It was only for her own good. "She'll enjoy going out once she gets used to it."

"All right. But I still don't see why I should pick you up first."

"Because I promised Deborah." He added a coaxing note to his voice. "She's just a little nervous, that's all."

"But you're not her big brother."

"I feel like it, though. After all, she's been Rachel's best friend for ten years. Rachel asked me to keep an eye on her."

"Oh. Well, I'm glad to hear that. I was afraid you were interested in her yourself. Though I guess Mariana takes care of you, doesn't she?" Richard asked with a laugh that held a note of envy.

"Mariana's a handful, all right," Jason agreed, without actually agreeing with the other man's assessment of his relationship with the redhead. The more he talked to Richard, the less he liked him.

"I'll calm Deborah's fears," Richard assured him, "and then I'll teach her how to enjoy life." His suggestive tone of voice left Jason in no doubt of his meaning. "Two years is a long time to go without."

Jason ended the conversation abruptly. The desire to punch Richard Estes in the nose was about to overpower him and he'd say something he would regret. He felt protective of Deborah, but he assured himself it was as he'd told Richard. She was Rachel's best friend.

And if that ape laid one finger on her, he'd be eating through a straw!

Four

"Manny, all you have to do is tell her how much you love her. Elizabeth feels the same way. She'd be crazy not to snap you up at once."

Elizabeth listened to Manny's doubts, removing her gold earring so she could hear his soft voice over the telephone more easily. Poor Manny, never having been married, was unsure of himself.

"Everything will be all right. Just be honest."

Movement caught her eye and she discovered her editor standing in the doorway of her cubicle, as he frequently did these days. It seemed she could hardly take a breath without him telling her how she could do it better!

She finished the conversation with Manny even as she mentally apologized to the sexy man in front of her. He really wasn't being quite so overbearing, but the changes he'd insisted on were impacting her life a great deal.

"Yes, Mr. Bridges? Did you want something?"

"Come on, Deborah, we're beyond the Mr. Bridges stage, aren't we?" he asked as he settled down in the chair in front of her desk.

"Fine . . . Jason," she finished with exasperation when he stared at her until she said his name. "Is that all you wanted?"

"Nope. I wanted to tell you I liked the changes you made in your column."

Relief and joy filled her. His words did more for her than any compliment she'd ever received. "Really, Jason?"

His smile broadened. "Really, Deborah."

"Then—" Deborah began, hope burgeoning in her, but she was interrupted by a young man sticking his head in her cubicle.

"Deborah, are you free for lunch? We could—oh, hello, Mr. Bridges. I didn't realize—I'll catch you later, Deborah."

"What was he doing down here?" Jason asked, frowning.

"That was Scott Hubbard. He's a sports reporter."

"I know who he is, Deborah, but the Sports Department is two floors up. This isn't his area." He glared at her.

Deborah refused to meet his gaze as she murmured, "He mentioned something about lunch."

Jason gave a non-committal grunt and asked, "What were you about to say?"

"I wondered—that is, if you're satisfied with my column, then I guess Friday night isn't necessary." She tried to keep her voice casual, so he wouldn't realize how much she was dreading an evening spent in Richard Estes's company.

"No way, Deb."

Before she could argue with him, another man interrupted them. "Hey, Deborah, do you want to—uhoh, I'll talk to you later."

Jason stared at her. When she started to speak again, he beat her to it. "No, don't bother to identify one of my assistant editors to me. I did recognize him. I just didn't realize he had anything to do with your column."

"I didn't say he did."

"It's because of the way you're dressing, isn't it? The men are coming out of the woodwork, and I'm responsible." He sounded disgusted with himself.

"I'm not—not dressing seductively," she protested, looking down at her grey tweed jacket over a red silk blouse. "I'm dressed professionally," she added, determined to make her point.

Jason laughed. "Yeah. But, damn it, you're so beautiful, you attract men whether you're trying or not."

She felt her cheeks flushing and looked away from him.

"All right, let's get to a more important subject. I like the changes you've made, but that doesn't mean we're through reworking the column. And it also doesn't mean you can back out of Friday night."

"But, Jason—"

"You promised, Deborah."

She had. In a weak moment, or perhaps because of his manipulation, she wasn't sure which, she'd promised to spend a miserable evening with Richard . . . and Jason and Mariana.

"All right. But—"

"Good. I'll see you on Friday night."

He stood and strolled to her door and she breathed a sigh of relief. Every encounter with this man involved risk, because her reaction to him was becoming more and more uncontrollable.

Unfortunately, she relaxed too soon.

He paused and turned to stare at her. "Who were you talking to when I arrived?"

"What?" Was he going to give her a lecture on personal phone calls?

"You were telling someone to be honest. I just wondered if some man was feeding you a line."

"No. I was talking to a friend." She didn't work by the hour and she was getting tired of Jason thinking he had the right to know everything about her. In fact, it was of paramount importance that she kept some things secret.

"A man friend?"

"Yes," she muttered, but she lifted her chin and glared at him, determined not to give an inch.

"Okay," he replied mildly, surprising her. "Oh, by the way, be sure you dress up for Friday night. You shouldn't dress professionally."

"Thank you, Miss Manners. Or should I say Coco Chanel?" she retorted in frustration. "Surely I've demonstrated that I don't need any fashion tips."

He smiled ruefully. "Yeah, I guess you've proven your fashion expertise. In fact, with poor old Richard, you might ought to dress in a burlap sack. I'm not sure his heart could take much more stimulation after the reception."

"Jason—" she began in exasperation, but he only waved his hand and disappeared. She certainly wasn't going to call him back just to get in the last word.

But she was sure of one thing. He'd have no complaints about what she wore Friday night.

She cleared her desk and prepared to leave. Jason liked her column and she'd already started on her next one. It was time to do some serious shopping . . . again.

"It was good to see Deb the other night," Paul said as he served himself some vegetables.

"Yes, it was," Rachel agreed.

Paul looked sharply at his wife. Rachel sounded distracted. "Is everything all right?"

She jumped as if he'd pinched her. "Yes, of course. Why wouldn't it be?"

He could name half a dozen reasons. Jason's return would do for a start. But most of all, for the past couple of years, Rachel had been consumed with getting pregnant. Since they'd lost their baby, she seemed to think of nothing else.

"What did you do today?"

"I went shopping with Deb."

"Really? Shopping for anything in particular? And how much damage did you do to my budget?" He was teasing, but her family was wealthy, and he was always conscious that he didn't make the same kind of money.

She smiled at him. "I didn't buy anything. We were shopping for something for a date Deb has Friday night."

Paul set down his fork and stared at his wife. "Deb has a date Friday night? I thought she didn't—"

"She didn't. She told me she hasn't dated at all since Randall's death." Rachel seemed lost in thought again.

"Who's the lucky guy?"

"Richard Estes."

"Too bad. I was hoping Jason might—" He shouldn't have mentioned that idea he realized just a little too late.

Rachel beamed at him. "Oh! I'm so glad you said that. I've been hoping the same thing, but I didn't want to say anything in case you thought I was butting in where I shouldn't."

"Now, honey, you're probably right. I mean, Jason's a big boy. He can—"

"No, he can't. He hasn't shown any talent at all in settling down and finding a nice girl. He wants to go back to every dirty little war he can find!" she finished vehemently.

"Different things tempt different people."

His beloved wife stared at him, anxiety in her eyes. "Do you ever feel that way?"

He jumped up from the table and pulled her into his arms. "Never, Rachel. I love you more than life itself."

She melted into his embrace, wrapping her arms around his neck.

Rachel's attempts to become pregnant had turned their lovelife into a marathon time and temperature schedule. The last time they'd come together spontaneously was too long ago to remember. He swept her up into his arms.

"What are you doing?" she whispered as she trailed kisses down his cheek.

"Making love to my wife," he assured her with a grin.

"But dinner—"

"Sweetheart, I've got a hunger carrots just won't satisfy." And she never once worried about her temperature!

* * *

Deborah stared at herself in the mirror. She'd chosen her outfit for the evening with Jason in mind. He was forcing her into this evening's outing, sure she couldn't handle dating. Well, she was going to show him.

The baby blue mohair sweater and matching skirt she'd chosen clung lovingly to her figure. The color made her eyes appear large, and she thought its softness would invite touch.

The cowl neckline was even more devilish, allowing the wearer to pull the neckline down both shoulders, showing a wide expanse of skin, if she dared. She did.

Her hair was loose, curling and dancing around her head. She took extra care with her makeup, keeping it light, but playing up her blue eyes.

She wasn't going to leave the maddening Jason Bridges in any doubt about her ability to handle dating in the nineties.

When she opened the door to the two gentlemen involved in her outing, she realized her mistake.

It wasn't that her appearance was lost on Jason. His eyes widened and she watched with satisfaction as he visibly swallowed. He wouldn't say anything, of course, like admitting he was wrong. But she saw the fire in his eyes, the tensing of his body.

No, her mistake was in forgetting Richard.

The man practically drooled on her as he took her hand. Where Jason recognized her appearance as a challenge, Richard saw it as an invitation, a demonstration of her interest in him.

Yes, a definite mistake.

"You look wonderful," Richard said, beaming. And breathing heavily.

Deborah murmured thank you and looked at Jason. She wanted to plead with him to stop the evening now. She'd made her point, hadn't she?

Instead of responding to the plea in her gaze, he stepped back. "Ready to go? Mariana is waiting for us."

She caught her breath. Of course, Mariana. "Yes, I'm ready."

Richard immediately took her arm and led her to his car. The care with which he installed her in the passenger side, using every opportunity to stroke her skin, didn't bode well for the evening. By the time they'd picked up Mariana, Deborah was on the verge of a headache. And her hands were already tired from meeting Richard's at every turn.

In the back seat, Jason seemed a more willing participant to Mariana's coziness. Deborah fought the urge to turn and stare at the couple. It was none of her business.

When they took their seats in the theater, Deborah ended up between the two men, with Mariana on the other side of Jason. Deborah shifted toward Jason as much as she dared, trying not to make her aversion to her date too obvious. Richard draped his arm behind her head and leaned toward her.

"I like these action flicks," he whispered hotly in her ear and then kissed it.

Ugh! Deborah fought the urge to take a tissue out of her purse and wipe her ear.

When the lights went off, Richard's arm dropped from the chair to her shoulders. Immediately, his hands began an exploration of her shoulder and arm, stroking her skin. She prayed the film would grab his attention away from her.

No such luck.

About an hour into the movie, Richard's hand moved from her arm to her breast. She immediately surged to her feet, grabbed her purse and tried to slide past Richard.

"Where are you going?"

"To the ladies' room," she hurriedly whispered and escaped into the aisle.

She spent about fifteen minutes in the ladies' room, fiddling with her hair and makeup, and, finally, leaning against the wall. When she eventually emerged into the lighted lobby, she was startled to discover Jason waiting patiently.

Frowning, she tried to think if she'd seen Mariana enter without paying attention. "Jason? I didn't see Mariana come in."

"Nope. She's watching the movie."

"Then what are you doing here?"

"Checking on you. Is anything wrong?" His worried look was balm to her irritation.

"No. I, uh, didn't find the movie interesting."

"Ah. Not an action fan?"

"Not particularly."

"I suppose you prefer those 'date' movies? The ones where the men are all sensitive and patient?" His eyes twinkled with silent laughter.

Though the corners of her lips quivered, she said solemnly, "Yes, I like fantasy movies."

He chuckled out loud. "I guess you put me in my place." When she only smiled and didn't move, he asked, "Aren't you going back into the movie?"

"I don't really want to. Why don't you tell Richard I'll meet the three of you out here when it's over." She didn't want to submit herself to Richard's pawing again. Nor did she want to admit to any problems to Jason, since he was her boss. He might decide she couldn't handle difficulties in dating. After all, that was the reason for this torture in the first place.

"I'm not too interested in the film, either. But I'll go tell the other two where we are. Wait here."

"But Jason—" She gave up when he'd already disappeared into the darkened theater again. Finding a bench in the lobby, she waited for him to return.

He was back quickly, a satisfied smile on his face.

"Any problems?" she asked.

"Nope. Except for the guy behind Richard. He complained that I was blocking his view." Before she could ask any more questions, he was off again, this time to the refreshment center, saying, over his shoulder, "Save my place."

When he returned, he hold two sodas and a tub of popcorn. "I love movie popcorn. Do you?"

"It's one of my favorite things."

"And is Richard one of your favorite things?"

"Sneak attack?" she asked, knowing he would understand her meaning, asking about her date as if it ranked right up there with movie popcorn. After all, her feelings about Richard were none of his business.

He acknowledged her reaction with a grin. "Just curious."

She wanted the conversation to take a more impersonal direction. "So, if this film doesn't thrill you, what kind do you like?"

"Good films."

Rolling her eyes, she tried again. "That's a cop-out answer and you know it."

"No, it's not. I liked *Star Wars,* but I'm not a real science fiction fan. *Jurassic Park* was exciting, but generally I don't go for fantasy. Some date movies are good, but not all of them. Westerns get me excited, but not all of them. Good comedies, but I'm not fond of slapstick. You see?"

She couldn't argue with anything he'd said, since she felt about the same way. "I see."

"That tells me a lot."

"What do you mean?"

He held out the popcorn and she popped several kernels into her mouth. "You haven't given me anything to go on about your tastes."

"I didn't know you were interested."

His gaze focused on hers and they stared at each other before she finally blinked and looked away. Then he simply said, "I'm interested."

She wasn't sure they were talking about movies. In fact, she almost caught her breath, hoping. Then, bringing her surprising thoughts under control, she used his words. "I like good films."

"No fair!" he protested, a grin on his face.

"Yes, it is. I can't argue with anything you said. Except maybe westerns."

"You don't like westerns?" he asked, horrified.

"Well, a few of them. But there aren't too many good roles for women in most westerns."

"Ah, you mean where the cowboy kisses his horse instead of the lady at the end?"

"Yes."

"No one said cowboys were bright," he commented with a shrug of his shoulders.

"Silly me to ask, after seeing you with Mariana." She regretted her words, but it was too late to take them back. All she could do was work at keeping the blush from her cheeks.

"That was a low blow."

"No, that was a fact. It's not as if the two of you sit on opposite sides of the car." Why couldn't she keep her mouth shut? She was only compounding the problem.

"Well, when a man is as irresistible as I am, these things happen," he assured her, a cocky grin on his face. But the laughter in his eyes told her he wasn't taking himself seriously.

She could only grin at him.

Unfortunately, she also knew, cocky or not, what he said was true. From the first minutes she'd seen him, in spite of being buried in remorse, she'd recognized that spark that draws women. Jason could be in a desert and he'd end up in a harem.

"Not that you do too badly yourself," he added.

"Maybe I did get a little carried away tonight," she admitted.

"Well, I think we can help the problem a little if we pull

your, uh, top back over your shoulders." He followed his words with a gentle touch, urging her sweater over her skin. "What do you think you're doing?" Richard demanded.

Five

It took all of Jason's diplomatic skills, and he had a lot of talent in that area, to smooth Richard's ruffled feathers. He wasn't quite as successful with Mariana, but he continued to work on her in the car.

The sound of long, hot kisses from the back seat made Deborah's headache no longer a lie.

By the time they reached the restaurant, Deborah decided the disastrous date would live in infamy. At least in her mind. To distract herself, she composed a reply to a letter she'd received earlier in the week from a lady who was intimidated by expensive restaurants.

"Need some help with the menu?" Richard asked, leaning toward her.

"No, thank you, I've dined here several times. I'm going to have the *coq au vin.*"

Mariana, of course, who played the helpless beauty to perfection, was demanding Jason's opinion of every item on the menu. Deborah gritted her teeth.

When the waiter arrived at their table to take their order, Richard attempted to give it in French. Since the waiter was a home-grown Texas boy and Richard's French was atrocious, it was all Deborah could do to keep from giggling. Her gaze met Jason's, full of silent laughter, and she quickly looked away.

"Oh, Richard, that was so impressive!" Mariana cooed. "Are you going to order in French, Jason?"

"No, I don't think I'll try it this evening." He smiled at the waiter. "The lady will have *Boeuf bouguignon* and I'll have Beef Wellington."

"Very good, *M'sieu,*" the boy answered in his best impression of a snooty French waiter. Deborah and Jason exchanged a smile.

Deborah had minored in French in college and could only imagine the grimace on her professor's face had he heard Richard mangle the beautiful language. She changed the subject to the movie.

The conversation hopscotched all over the place after that. Curiously, Richard and Mariana agreed more than they did with either of their dates. When the subject of local sports came up, Jason, new to the area, had a number of questions, and only Deborah could supply any answers.

"I don't watch sports," Richard assured the other man. "They're a waste of time."

"Yes, they are," Mariana agreed. "So boring."

Deborah supplied Jason with information about the local baseball team, the Texas Rangers, who were in Florida for spring training at the moment. She surprised him, however, when she mentioned the local hockey teams.

"Hockey? Ice hockey? In Texas?"

"Yes, they started up a couple of years ago. Of course, two of the teams are minor league, but I've heard the games are fun."

"You've never been?"

"No. No, I haven't gone out much lately." She looked away from the unspoken apology in his gaze.

"I suppose I could get tickets," Richard began, frowning, "if you really want to go, but I'd prefer the opera."

"That's all right, Richard. I wouldn't want you to do that." Since she had no intention of going out with him again, whether to a hockey game or an opera, she was glad when his frown disappeared.

"Oh, good. The Charity Ball is coming up. Have you ever attended? Everyone who's important is there. Great contacts," he assured Jason earnestly. "Mrs. Carson is a big backer."

Mariana nodded wisely. "And you mustn't cross Mrs. Carson. My mother always supports the same charities, because if Mrs. Carson thinks you're not doing your part, she'll ruin you."

"I see," Jason said gravely, but his eyes were dancing with laughter, and Deborah raised her napkin to her lips to hide the smile growing there.

By the time dinner ended, Deborah was exhausted. Her less than honest responses to her companions took a lot of effort.

Even worse, Richard's hand had strayed under the table numerous times, touching Deborah's knee and once even her thigh. Though she'd pushed his hand away, he didn't seem to understand her response. It was a relief when they headed home.

"Why don't we drop the ladies off first, Estes?" Jason suggested. "I'd like to talk business for a few minutes."

"That would be nice," Deborah hurriedly agreed when she saw the stubbornness on Richard's face. "I'm afraid I'm not used to such a full evening. I've been a real stay-at-home the last couple of years." It didn't take much effort to smile wearily at the man beside her.

"Okay," he conceded, but he was grumpy the rest of the drive.

"There's no need to walk me to the door, Richard," she said, as they pulled into her circle driveway. "It's just a couple of steps."

He said nothing but opened his door. Deborah slipped from the car after a brief goodbye to the other two before he could open it for her.

His determined hold on her elbow as they reached the door warned Deborah that his idea of their leavetaking would not be to her taste.

"I'll call you tomorrow and we'll make plans of our own. We're too old for double-dating," he said firmly.

She smiled but said nothing, watching him carefully. When he dipped his head for a goodnight kiss, she turned her face so that the kiss landed on her cheek.

"Thank you for a lovely evening, Richard," she added as she slipped the key into the door. Without ever looking at him, she closed the door behind her, flipped off the alarm system, and plopped down in the first chair she came to.

Jason was wrong. She didn't need any practice for tonight's date. A jerk was a jerk. And Richard qualified, hands down. In fact, he qualified *with* his hands. She thought he had eight of them.

"So, tell me all about it," Rachel prompted after they'd been seated at the restaurant, their packages on the empty chairs at their table. Unable to meet on Friday as planned, Rachel had suggested Monday, and after shopping all morning, they both were ready for a break.

"All about what?"

"Don't pretend to be Miss Innocent. About the date Friday night. Did you like Richard?"

At least that was a question Deborah could answer. "He's a—an interesting man but we didn't have much in common."

"Ah. So you won't go out with him again?"

"Maybe he won't ask."

Rachel giggled. "Sure! I believe that. After that dress you wore to the reception, you'll have to be brutal to discourage him."

Deborah refused to admit Rachel might be right. Richard had certainly said he would call. And he had. But she'd let the answering machine take his calls all weekend. She could only hope he'd realize just how miserable their date was and change his mind.

"What did you think of my big brother and the redhead?" Rachel asked, leaning forward.

That was a question Deborah had no intention of answering. Desperately searching for an evasive answer, she discovered Rachel looking over her shoulder.

"Hi, Paul. I'm so glad you could join us. And Jason. What a surprise."

Deborah closed her eyes. She should've known. Rachel had been the one to suggest lunch now. And she'd chosen the restaurant. Deborah opened her eyes to find Jason staring down at her. She nodded and turned to smile at Paul.

"This *is* a surprise." She wanted to make sure Jason knew *she* hadn't planned their meeting.

"I wanted to be sure Rachel wasn't going to force us into bankruptcy," Paul assured her with a grin, moving packages to the floor from the chair next to his wife. "Though I think I might be too late if all these are her purchases."

"None of them is mine," Rachel said triumphantly. "Though I did see a blouse I may go back and buy. It can be your birthday gift to me."

"And how expensive is my taste?" he asked, but the teasing smile on his lips told Deborah he wasn't worried.

"Very," Rachel drawled and leaned over to kiss him.

Deborah looked away and found her gaze locking with Jason's. She hurriedly stared at the menu.

"Cut it out, you two. You're making us feel like fifth wheels," Jason growled. "What did you buy, Deborah?"

Though her cheeks tingled with heat, she kept her gaze on the menu. "Work clothes."

Jason groaned.

"What's wrong, brother. Don't you want your employees to look good?" Rachel demanded.

"If Deborah looks any better, we'll never get the paper out on time."

She glared at him. "You're being ridiculous. Besides—"

"I know, I know. It's all my fault."

The waiter's arrival at their table forced an end to the conversation and Deborah was relieved. When he'd taken their orders and departed, she searched for an innocuous topic in which Paul and Rachel would have an interest.

"Friday evening, Richard mentioned the Charity Ball. Are you two going this year?"

Paul grimaced even as Rachel answered. "We've skipped it the last few years, but Daddy says we should be there for the sake of the paper. You, too, Jason."

"I think Dad and Mom should fly in for it," Jason said. "If we're going to suffer, they should, too."

"Sssh!" Rachel quickly responded. "Don't let anyone hear you describing the social event of the year as suffering."

Jason rolled his eyes and Paul nodded. Jason then looked at Deborah. "Are you going?"

"Did Richard ask you?" Rachel chimed in before Deborah could answer.

"She's not going anywhere with him!" Jason replied, not even looking at Deborah.

"Thank you so much for making all my decisions for me, Mr. Bridges." She glared at him again.

"She gets formal when she's mad at me," Jason explained *sotto voce* to the others, but the twinkle in his eyes as he looked at her invited her laughter. She pressed her lips firmly together to hold back her response.

The man had already prodded her into two mistakes, dressing sexier than she would have normally. She wasn't going to suffer through another date with Richard just to score points off Jason Bridges!

"Just what *did* happen Friday night?" Rachel asked since Deborah remained silent.

"Nothing," Deborah said quietly.

At the same time, Jason growled, "He put his hands all over her."

Her suppressed anger escaped her control. "Do you mind? I'd rather not discuss my personal life in public. Besides, you don't have much room to complain!"

"What do you mean?" he whipped back.

"You and Mariana didn't have a lot of time for conversation in the back seat." She regretted her words as soon as they were out. She didn't want him to know she'd noticed his movements on that ill-fated date.

When she got up her nerve to look at him in the silence that followed, she was surprised to discover his cheeks were red. Of course, Paul's knowing chuckle didn't help matters. Jason cleared his throat, as if about to speak.

"I apologize," Deborah hastily said. "I shouldn't have commented on your—your behavior. Could we please just discuss something else?" She looked at Rachel, pleading with her eyes for some assistance.

"So, how's the paper shaping up, Jason?" Rachel asked, and even tried to quell the grin that teased the corners of her lips.

Though his first few words were stiff, Jason responded to his sister's question and gradually relaxed, explaining the changes he was making at the *Fort Worth Daily*. Paul helped keep the conversation going with a few astute questions, and Deborah relaxed also.

Though Jason watched her out of the corner of his eye, the rest of the lunch conversation was impersonal, covering current events and problems at the paper. At last, the men said they had to return to their respective offices and Deborah heaved a sigh of relief.

"Are you coming into the office today?" Jason asked her before they parted in front of the restaurant.

"No. I'm ahead of schedule. Today I'm concentrating on shopping."

He nodded and Deborah expected him to leave. Instead, he reached out and caught hold of her chin. "Did you buy anything blue?"

Shocked, she stepped back, pulling from his grasp. "Bl-blue? I don't think so."

"Why do you ask, Jason?" Rachel asked, her gaze on the two of them.

"I like her in blue," he replied, but his gaze never left Deborah.

She stared at him, wide-eyed, unsure how to respond. He reached out and caressed one cheek with a knuckle and then walked away, leaving her rigid, fighting the response the simple touch had drawn from her.

"My, my, my," Rachel said with a grin. "He likes you in blue. That's quite an admission from my big brother."

Jason strode down the street, his hands shoved in his pockets, irritated with himself, not even noticing when Paul caught up with him. He hadn't intended to ask about her purchases. He hadn't intended to ask her to buy something blue. He hadn't intended to touch her.

But he had.

He didn't need anyone to tell him Deborah was a home and hearth lady, one of those women who wanted marriage, children, a husband who came home at a regular time each evening. The exact opposite of what he wanted. Her life sounded too much like his parents'.

But, damn it, she was packaged all wrong.

He didn't think of milk and cookies, babies or station wagons when he looked at her. Instead his mind wandered to lace, silk, warm scented skin. He pictured two bodies entwined—always touching, sparks flying—

"Deb's quite a looker," Paul said, staring straight ahead, trying to appear disinterested.

Jason had forgotten his brother-in-law walking beside him. His words demanded a response. "Yeah."

"She's also, uh, kind of special."

"Should Rachel be worried?" Jason asked, hoping to end the probing.

Paul almost tripped over his own feet as he hurried to deny Jason's words. "No! I didn't mean—"

"I know you didn't. You're trying to find out what I think about Deborah, probably on strict orders from my beloved sister."

Paul had the grace to blush.

Before he could try again to fulfill his wife's commission, Jason said, "Look, the woman's beautiful, but she wants a conventional life. I'm heading back to my old job in a few months."

This time Paul came to a complete halt. "Jason, you know you're my favorite in-law, but—but don't hurt Deb. She's been through a rough time."

"She already knows I'll be leaving. It's no secret." Jason's jaw squared and his lips pressed together, letting Paul know he didn't appreciate the warning.

"It's—it's Rachel, too."

"What do you mean?"

Paul stood there, his head down, as if considering his answer.

"Paul?" Jason prompted.

"Since we lost the baby, having a child is all Rachel can think about. We've visited doctors, scheduled our—well, you know. Worried about it all the time." He looked up at Jason, concern in his eyes. "But since Rachel's found Deb again, she's relaxed, thinking about other things." He shrugged his shoulders. "I just want her to be happy."

"I know you do. And that's why you're *my* favorite in-law. I'll try not to screw things up, okay? Deborah and I have a professional friendship. And that's all."

Even though he read the disbelief in Paul's eyes, Jason pasted on a smile and started walking. Fast. He didn't want any more questions.

After leaving Paul outside the building, he reached his

office, only to be handed a stack of phone messages by his secretary. "Mr. Estes has called several times, Mr. Bridges. I told him you'd return his calls, but he keeps calling back."

Just who he wanted to talk to. "Thanks, Brenda. I'll call him right now so he won't pester you to death."

What did the jerk want? He certainly wasn't going to arrange any more dates for him. There must be someone else Deborah could date to gain experience. He couldn't think of anyone, but there must be some man who wouldn't try to hustle her to bed as soon as the introductions were made.

"Hello, Richard. This is Jason Bridges."

"About time!" Richard growled. "I'm worried about Deborah. I tried to get her all weekend but her answering machine was on. And she hasn't come into the paper today. Do you think she's all right?"

Jason leaned back in his chair, a smile on his face. He was going to enjoy this conversation. "She's fine. I just had lunch with her."

Silence heavy with tension came through the telephone wire. "You just had lunch with her? Is she at work now?"

"No. She and my sister are shopping today."

More silence.

"Okay, sorry to bother you. I'll just catch her later."

"No problem. 'Bye." Actually, he never wanted to talk to the man again. He'd had to come up with some business talk after they'd dropped Mariana off Friday night, and he'd gotten his fill of Richard Estes.

Apparently Deborah had, too. He didn't want to think about why that fact pleased him. He just knew it did. In spite of her protest at lunch today, she had no intention of going out with the man again.

A sudden thought stopped him. Unless she really had been away all weekend. He remembered that call she'd had Thursday. From a man. Had Deborah spent the weekend with a man? Another man?

Six

Deborah heard the phone ringing as she opened the door from the garage. She put her packages on the kitchen table and reached for the wall phone, then plopped down in a chair. She was exhausted.

"Deborah? This is Richard. I've been trying to get you all weekend. Are you all right?"

"Hello, Richard. Yes, I'm fine. I'm sorry I missed you." Thank goodness he couldn't see her face or he'd know she was lying.

"I just wanted to talk to you, make plans for this weekend." The urgency in his voice was replaced by a warmth she didn't want to hear.

"Oh, I hope I haven't caused you to reorganize your plans. I'm afraid I'm tied up this weekend."

"I thought you didn't date." Irritation tinged his words.

"I don't, Richard. That is, I enjoyed our evening out, but—but I'm really not ready for the social scene just yet. I'm afraid I'd be a wet blanket."

"You'll warm up once we're alone. I've been told I'm a real turn-on."

Deborah almost groaned aloud. Just what she needed. A man who believed all his own press reviews. "Sorry, Richard, but I don't intend to go out with you." She didn't add any excuses. A grown man who used the term *turn-on* to describe himself didn't deserve the niceties.

"I don't think you're being fair, Deborah. After all, I spent a lot of money Friday night. And all I got was one little kiss."

"I'll be glad to pay for my share of the evening, Richard. How much do I owe you?"

"Come on, Deborah, you know that's not what I want. I can afford an expensive evening. But I thought you'd, you know, cooperate a little. Like Mariana."

"Our conversation is over, Richard. Goodbye."

He was still talking when she hung up the receiver, but she didn't care. He made her sick to her stomach. She hadn't dated a jerk like that since the ninth grade when she had a crush on a football star.

When the phone rang again before she could move away, she was too angry with the man to let the machine answer it. "Don't call me again!" she spit into the phone.

"Why? This is the first time I've called," a deep voice said, laughter lurking in his reasonable response.

"Jason. I—I thought you were someone else."

"Let me guess. Could it be our friend Richard?"

"He's not *my* friend, and it's your fault that I had to suffer through that horrible evening." She sat back down in the chair, cradling the receiver against her shoulder, enjoying the warm rasp of his voice.

"It wasn't all bad. The food was good."

"But the conversation wasn't. I don't know which was worse, Richard trying to speak French, or Mariana raving about his accent."

Jason chuckled. "I thought you were going to break into giggles."

"If I had, it would've been your fault. You tempted me to laugh every time you gave me one of those knowing looks."

"That's because I like to hear you laugh."

"But Mariana might never have forgiven you."

"Darn." The sardonic tone of his voice demonstrated how

little he might care if Mariana lost interest in him. It raised a lot of interesting questions Deborah decided she shouldn't ask.

"Why did you call?" A much safer topic.

"Just to make sure you put Estes out of his misery. He called me at the office about twenty times today. My secretary hates the sound of his voice now."

"Join the crowd."

"That bad, huh? So, did you tell him to get lost?"

Deborah was relieved he hadn't heard her previous conversation. "I hope I have better manners than that." She didn't, but Jason didn't need to know that.

"He doesn't deserve manners. The man's an idiot, except for one thing."

"What thing?"

"His taste in women." His voice was low, sexy.

Deborah closed her eyes and swallowed. Finally, she said, "Well, he won't be calling you or me anymore, I suspect."

"Good. Of course, that leaves us with a problem."

"What problem?"

"Your social education. We need to find some nice guy who won't hound you to death to take you out."

Deborah felt her anger rising and tried to keep it under control. "Thank you, Mr. Bridges, but that won't be necessary. I can assure you I have enough social expertise to handle the column."

"Deborah, we're right back where we started. I really think, for your writing's sake, we'll have to—"

"Stop it! I'll—I'll find someone to date. I do not need you to act as procurement officer!"

"Whew! You do have a temper, don't you?" Jason teased, chuckling.

"Only with bossy men!"

She never pierced his armor. He only laughed before saying, "Okay, okay, I'll back off and give you a chance. Let me know when you find someone."

"Oh, don't worry," Deborah cooed, "I'll be sure you're the first to know." Then she slammed down the phone.

"How do you want to celebrate your birthday?" Paul asked Rachel, cuddling her against him on the sofa.

She reached up to kiss his chin. "Mmmm, I can think of several ways."

"I'm all in favor of that, sweetheart, but we don't have to wait until your birthday," he assured her, pulling her even closer.

Sometime later, in their kingsize bed, Rachel spoke again. "That was wonderful." She giggled. "And it wasn't even scheduled."

"I know. And if that's what happens when I talk about your birthday, you're going to get sick and tired of hearing about it."

"Why don't we have dinner here for my birthday—for four?" Rachel asked, not responding to his teasing.

"Uh-oh. I think I see where this is leading, Rachel, and you're making a mistake."

"No, I'm not. They're perfect for each other."

Paul flung his arm over his eyes. "Rachel, your brother is not going to stay here in Fort Worth. He's already got plans to go back to the Middle East in just a few months."

"He won't go if he falls in love with Deborah. I'll just give her a call."

A few minutes later she returned to the bedroom where her husband hadn't moved. "Paul?"

"Yes?"

"There's been a slight change of plans."

He pushed himself up, fixing a pillow behind him. "Now what have you done, Rachel?"

"Nothing, really. I just invited Deb, but she made me promise it wouldn't be just the four of us, and, well, I kind of assured her it was a party."

Paul groaned. "A party? So now we have to spend the evening with a lot of people we don't even want to see? Aw, Rachel!"

"It won't be that bad. I'll just make it a few couples, just people we like."

"But, honey, it's your birthday. I don't want you doing a lot of work."

"Oh, pooh! It won't be so bad. I'll have it catered. That can be your birthday present to me." She smiled angelically.

"Wait a minute. I thought I bought you that expensive blouse."

"Oh, I forgot," she assured him with a grin, knowing he didn't believe her. "Well, how about I ask Mom and Dad for the blouse."

"I got a better idea. Why don't you ask them for the party? I don't think the blouse is going to cost anywhere near that much!" He reached for her even as he answered her suggestion and soon there was no more talk at all.

Jason lay on several pillows in his unmade bed, dressed in sweats and tennis shoes, watching the news. He'd jogged late tonight, after a frustrating conversation with Mariana.

The woman wanted more than he was willing to give. Placating her was taking more time than he had. But he needed someone to escort to the social obligations he had as editor of the paper.

Not that Mariana was ideal for such a role. The woman was too self-absorbed. At a reception Sunday evening, she'd tried to nibble on his ear while he was talking to the mayor. This evening, she was insisting they spend Friday night alone.

Mariana had been making it clear that she expected more from their relationship than a few goodnight kisses. His lack of response to such a sexually potent package would worry him if it weren't for one thing.

He was responding, all right. But not to Mariana.

There had been a flare of lust when he first met Mariana. After all, she was beautiful. But it hadn't taken long for him to realize that only her body had any sex appeal. Her mind was just so much barren wasteland.

About the same time, he'd taken Deborah to lunch. From that moment on, his head had been engaged. The night of the reception, his body had caught up and passed his mind. The damnable thing about it was that Deborah would be perfect as his companion. She had more class in her little finger than Mariana would ever have.

But he wouldn't mislead her. And he wouldn't marry her. Marriage didn't fit into his plans. That made the two of them incompatible.

So, now he had to figure out a way to stall Mariana, or go to bed with her. Frankly, he didn't think he could do that with Deborah in his head.

He pounced on the phone when it rang, driven by a sudden hope that Deborah might be calling him. "Oh. Hi, sis."

"You sound disappointed. Were you expecting Mariana?"

"No, I wasn't. What's up?"

"Well, my birthday's coming up—"

"You've already hinted and I'm going to buy you a present," he assured her, a grin on his face.

"That's not what I meant, but if you want to give me any hints?"

"Nope."

"That's 'cause you don't know what you're buying. Anyway, I'm calling to tell you I'm having a birthday party Friday night, and, of course, I expect you to be there."

"Friday? Your birthday isn't until Sunday."

"I know, but Friday is the party. You'll be there?"

"I've already made plans with Mariana. May I bring her?" At least that would keep them from being alone all evening.

"Yes, of course."

"Rachel, why did you fix me up with Mariana?" He'd pondered that question several times since he was sure his sister didn't even like the woman.

"Why, because she's beautiful," Rachel replied, suddenly sounding out of breath. "I have to go. Be here at seven."

Before he could answer, she'd hung up.

Wednesday, Deborah was putting the final touches on the column for Friday's paper. A month ago, she would've been pleased with its contents. Now, she sighed with disgust. Jason was right. Her column did sound like it was written by a little old lady. But she'd gone through all the letters she'd received this week. There wasn't anything unusual or earth shattering.

"Unhappy?"

She didn't have to look up to know it was Jason at her door. She hadn't seen him since the luncheon Monday, but she had been listening for his voice ever since. "Not exactly."

"Then why the sigh?"

She looked at him, taking in his sexy image. Today he was wearing a pin-striped suit, crisp white shirt and a tie that was a blend of colors. And he looked more appealing than any man had a right to.

"I just don't think you're going to like my column this week, Jason. I tried, but all the letters are about *manners!*"

One eyebrow shot up over his hazel eyes and he grinned. "You're kidding."

"No. Look for yourself." She shoved forward a pile of letters.

He sat down in the chair across from her and picked up several letters, skimming them. "I'll be damned. Here's a lady wanting to know about drinking tea while wearing her gloves? Where has she been the last forty or fifty years? Where did you get these?"

"They came in the mail. What can I do? I can't make up something."

"So what did you choose?"

She reluctantly handed him her column.

After reading it, he looked up at her, disbelief in his gaze. "Dentures? You answered a letter about dentures?"

"It's more than that," she said defensively. "The man is worried about his date being upset when he reveals that he has dentures."

While she protested, he'd been reading her response. With a chuckle, he said, "Not a bad answer, Townsend."

"Thank you," she murmured, trying to ignore the warmth his praise brought. "I tried to remember to keep it humorous without laughing *at* anyone."

"The second one's got to go," he said abruptly, washing away that warmth.

"But I don't have anything better to go in its place."

"Don't you have some letters you saved from previous weeks, something we could put in as if you'd just now gotten to it?"

"No, not really."

"What about that phone call the other day?"

"What call?" Deborah asked but avoided his gaze. She knew but she had no intention of using that letter.

"The one you said was from a man."

"It was personal." She looked up to see him drilling her with his gaze.

"Where were you this weekend?"

The sudden shift in conversation left Deborah floundering. "What?"

"Estes said he tried to reach you all weekend, but your machine was on."

"Oh, that. I was home. I just didn't want to talk to him." Something in his face made her ask, "Why?"

"No reason. Now, who was the letter from?"

His persistence irritated her. "I'll look for another letter, but it won't be that one. It's personal, and you have no business asking me about it."

"Don't get huffy. I just thought we could use it. I know, we'll get someone here to write a letter. That would be legitimate. There's nothing that says your letters have to come through the post office."

"Of course not. But who would agree to write a letter?"

He reached for her phone. "Let me make a phone call."

She nodded and he quickly dialed his office. With only a few words, his secretary had agreed to ask some of the secretaries and young reporters to gather in his office for a discussion about the dating scene at four o'clock.

"Now," he said with a self-satisfied grin, "all you have to do is show up and pick out some questions you can answer for the column." As he stood, he added, "In fact, I think you can throw out the dentures guy, too."

"No, I don't want to. I'm willing to write for a younger crowd, as long as I don't scare off the older ones. They're interested in romance, too. *And* they read more than young people."

"Okay. You've got a point. Dentures stays, but the other letter will be to a younger crowd. See you at four."

He left before Deborah remembered she meant to ask him *not* to attend the meeting.

As four o'clock approached, Deborah grew more and more nervous. In spite of her arguments with Jason, she wasn't at all sure she was qualified to give advice on today's dating scene. And she was about to be put to the test in front of the one person she was trying to convince of her knowledge.

She walked up the two floors to the Executive Suite, a pen and notepad clutched in sweaty fingers. Had dating changed that much? It hadn't felt like it Friday night. Richard hadn't shown any more class or poise than some of the freshmen she'd dated at the university.

Oh, well, she'd prepared a few questions to get the ball rolling. She crossed her fingers that it worked.

Jason welcomed her into his office and she found eight people of both sexes appearing to be between the ages of twenty and thirty-five.

She sat down in the chair he showed her. As he prepared to join them, she said, "Jason, perhaps it would be better if I took it from here. We don't want to take up your time."

"Nonsense, Deborah. I'll let you handle everything, of course, but I think I'll stay."

She ignored the laughter in his eyes as he sat down beside her and addressed the others. "We're trying to update our romance advice column a little, but we're not getting the letters we need to do that. Mr. Bridges thought you might help me out by talking about problems you've encountered while dating. Don't feel that you have to get too personal. But do you have questions or concerns?"

A dead silence followed. A few wary glances were exchanged, and several people shifted in their chairs. She could feel Jason's gaze.

"What do you think about honesty in a relationship? Is it okay to lie if you think it will keep the other person from being hurt?"

One young lady almost jumped from her chair as if electric volts had been charging through it. "No! It's never okay to lie!"

A young man beside her disagreed, and in no time, a vibrant conversation ensued. Deborah sat back and took notes, occasionally inserting a question when an issue had been talked out.

Two hours later, the atmosphere in the room was warm and friendly, even intense in a couple of instances. The first two speakers were showing an awareness of each other that amused Deborah. Until it reminded her of her wariness of Jason.

At that moment, Jason spoke up for the first time.

"Thanks a lot for coming. I hate to push you out the door, but I have an appointment."

Deborah stopped two people and asked them if they could write down a particular problem they'd discussed in letter form for tomorrow to use in the column. After agreeing, they slipped from the room until there was only her and Jason.

"Nice job, Deborah."

"Thank you, Jason. Do you agree now that I have enough social experience to write my column?"

He grinned. "I don't know. I thought you were going to lose your cool when that redhead asked which condoms were the best."

Deborah struggled for composure as she felt her cheeks grow warm. "I don't have a lot of experience in that area."

He opened his mouth and then shut it. "I don't think I'd better say that."

"What?"

"Nothing. Let's go."

"Where?"

"Dinner. I'm starved."

"I thought you had an appointment."

"I do. Dinner with you."

"Well, thank you for the gracious invitation, but I can't join you."

"Someone waiting at home?"

She turned away and then felt a warm hand on her shoulder.

"Damn it, Deborah, I forgot. I promise I wasn't trying to hurt you. I just thought I'd take you to dinner before asking you to do me a favor."

She sighed before saying, "Apology accepted. What favor?"

"Will you have dinner with me?"

"That's your favor?"

"Nope. That's the softening-up process before I ask the

favor. I promise it will be more enjoyable than Friday's dinner."

"It could hardly be less. All right, I'll agree to dinner, but I want to know what the favor is before I go."

Seven

"You really didn't have to buy me dinner just to get me to help you pick out a gift for Rachel," Deborah said an hour later as they were waiting for their food in one of Fort Worth's most famous Mexican restaurants, Joe T. Garcia's.

"I know. But I don't like to eat alone." Jason smiled at the picture she made, dressed for the office in a slim beige skirt and matching jacket over a sunny yellow blouse. She was a golden sunset against bright serapes and pinatas. "Have you come up with any ideas?"

"She's a real fan of Clint Black. You might buy her some tapes or a CD."

"I'd forgotten about that. Isn't he appearing at Billy Bob's sometime soon?" he asked, naming the largest country-western bar and entertainment center in town. Deborah shrugged her shoulders and he frowned in thought. "Yeah, I'm sure he is. Good idea, Deb. I'll get some tickets for her and a backstage pass."

"Can you do that?"

Jason's eyebrows soared. "Hey, you're talking to the editor of one of the local papers. Of course I can." Then he grinned wryly. "At least I hope so."

The waiter brought their food, and conversation was forgotten for several minutes.

Deborah paused to grin at him. "Thanks, Jason."

He looked at her, wondering what she could be thanking

him for. This was the best evening he'd had since he arrived in town. Relaxation, good food and even better company. "What?"

"Just—thanks for bringing me here. I haven't visited Joe T.'s since—in a while."

"You used to come here often?"

"Every special occasion. I love Mexican food."

"So you're not a wine and tablecloth kind of woman?" he teased, enjoying the warmth in her gaze.

"On occasion. But I like to let my hair down sometimes, too."

"Good." He turned his attention to his food again, hoping to dispel the happy complacency that was filling his heart. This woman was too good to be true. "What's your idea of a fun vacation?"

"Depends upon my mood. Water rafting and hiking are fun. So is a trip to New York to see the plays."

Damn. "And your favorite kind of movie?"

"I love romances and happy endings, but I also like comedies."

"I like cop movies." He hadn't meant to sound so pushy, but he was relieved to find something to argue over.

"You mean like the *Lethal Weapon* series? I liked those, too, but they were a little gory."

"I liked them just the way they were."

"Okay."

"I like to fish."

"Do you? Have you tried fishing around here? Lake Whitney is good," she suggested.

"How do you know?" He sounded too aggressive, but he thought he'd found a topic about which she'd know nothing.

"Oh, my dad used to take me fishing. And he still goes."

"I bet you don't bait your own hook."

"Not if you're using worms," she agreed with a smile.

When he didn't respond, she tilted her head to one side and said, "Are you trying to pick a fight with me?"

He jerked, dropping a bite of enchilada back onto his plate. "Don't be ridiculous. Why would I want to do that?"

"I don't know. It just seemed—never mind. Tell me about being a reporter, working in the hot spots of the world."

That he could do. He'd given lectures on the subject. It was safe to tell stories. They wouldn't be sharing if he gave a monologue.

An hour later, when they finally left the restaurant, he discovered he'd been wrong. Deborah had asked questions, made comments, drawn from him more than he'd ever told anyone else. She wanted to know his feelings, not just what happened. And he'd read in her eyes the empathy, the enjoyment, and what scared him most of all, the concern.

He'd promised Paul he'd keep his relationship with Deborah on a professional level. He was doing a damn poor job of keeping his promise.

Even worse, she tugged at his heart with her smile, her beauty, her intelligence. He had plans for the future, and those plans didn't include a wife and children. His father had settled for that lifestyle. *He* was going to travel the world.

All the way back to the paper, where she could pick up her car, Jason had little to say. Unfortunately, he discovered Deborah could be just as enjoyable maintaining silence as anyone he'd ever known.

When she opened the door to get out, he stopped her to make one last effort to shatter the rapport. "Need a ride Friday night? Mariana and I can stop by for you. She wanted to have me to herself, but I persuaded her to come to the party."

Deborah blinked several times before saying, "How nice for you. Thanks for the offer, but I believe I'll drive myself. Then if I want to leave early, I won't have to disturb your evening." She slid from the car and then bent down to say, "Oh, and thanks for the dinner, Jason. It was lovely."

Once she was behind the wheel of her car, the door locked and the motor running, Deborah released the breath she'd been holding. Waving to Jason, who was waiting for her to drive out of the parking lot, she set the car in motion.

How could you forget? He was Mariana's. Well, she was welcome to him. He was leaving. Deborah didn't want someone with wanderlust. She didn't want any man. She was just fine the way she was. She was perfectly happy. She had a full life. Men like Jason Bridges were a dime a dozen. *And I'm lying to myself.*

A tear eased down her cheek, followed by another. She *was* lying. Jason Bridges was special. But he wasn't for her.

She sniffed and dug into her purse with one hand for a tissue as she negotiated the downtown streets of Fort Worth. Thank goodness it wasn't rush hour.

She gulped deep breaths of air. Maybe she should be grateful to Jason. He'd already made her realize she'd been hiding from life. Now he'd shown her she could still be interested in the opposite sex. Damn! She should send him a thank you card!

The tears increased, and she swiped at her cheeks with the tissue. If the man kept on improving her life, she was going to have to shoot herself. She couldn't stand much more!

Anger at the trick life had played on her finally brought an end to her tears. But it didn't solve her problem. Jason Bridges had ripped a hole a mile wide in her heart and she was in pain.

All those years while Rachel had bragged about her big brother, Deborah had admired him. From a distance. Up close and personal, Jason was more than a friend's brother, more than a courageous reporter, more than a distant image.

He was warm, charming, exciting. He was damned lovable and she hated him!

A sigh shuddered through her as she pulled into her driveway. She only wished that were true, she finally admitted. She didn't hate him. But she didn't love him. Yet. Forewarned was forearmed.

No more dinners for two. No more chitchat. Everything from now on would be strictly business. Distant. Cool.

And no matter what else, she absolutely, positively would never think of him putting his arms around her, lowering those oh-so-masculine lips to hers, sweeping her up and heading for her bedroom. Oh, no. Definitely no more thoughts like that.

Mariana leaned across to his bucket seat and ran a well-manicured finger up Jason's arm to his jaw and stroked it slowly. "Why don't we leave early this evening? I'm sure Rachel won't mind. You've never shown me your apartment."

She pressed her full bosom against him, and Jason cleared his throat. "Rachel's my only sister, Mariana. She's pretty important to me."

Jerking away, she crossed her arms and glared at him. "I'm beginning to wonder what kind of man you are, Jason."

He was tempted to be honest with her, brutally honest, explaining that he just didn't have any interest in her, but he figured she'd spoil his sister's party. "Don't be silly, Mariana. I didn't say we had to be the last to leave."

She relented, putting her hand on his thigh. "It's just that I'm so impatient, Jason," she said breathlessly, squeezing. "We've been dating for *weeks!*"

Which gave him a pretty fair estimate of Mariana's expectations. Too bad he wasn't a nineteen-year-old. She wouldn't have had to wait even one night. But he'd grown wiser in the past fifteen years. He needed more than a spectacular body pressed against him to turn him on.

His mind drifted to Deborah. He hadn't seen her since Wednesday night. Today when he'd dropped by her office, it was vacant. He'd called her house this afternoon to offer her a ride again, just in case she'd changed her mind, but the answering machine had been on.

Would she wear the dress she'd worn to the reception? If she did, he wasn't sure he could hide his response. Hell, she'd looked just as sexy to him in her beige suit. And the thought of what she'd look like in the bedroom sent his blood pressure soaring through—

"I knew you were interested," Mariana cooed, showing her awareness of his body's reaction.

Jason reached down and removed her hand from his leg. "Better not disrupt the driver's attention, Mariana. We want to arrive safely."

"Oh, yes, so we can leave soon," she whispered as he parked the car.

As soon as he entered his sister's house, he looked for Deborah. Rachel greeted him with a kiss and passed him and Mariana on to Paul, who escorted them to the living room.

"Deborah's not here yet?" Jason whispered to his brother-in-law as Mariana greeted friends.

"Haven't seen her."

Half an hour later, Jason was growing worried. He was about to suggest Rachel call Deborah when the two ladies appeared in the entrance to the living room. They were a striking contrast, one brunette, vibrant, laughing, the other a cool blonde, smiling but distant.

He frowned. Where were the sexy clothes she'd worn on the other two occasions? Tonight she was dressed in a dark purple tunic and leggings, only the barest hint of her curves visible. Her hair was smooth and pulled back with combs, her makeup subdued.

He couldn't take his eyes off her.

"Everyone's here now," Rachel called, over the conversations, "and I want to open presents before we eat." They all sat down as Rachel settled behind the pile of gifts. Even though the invitation had said no presents, most people had brought a small gift of some kind.

Jason grabbed an easy chair, but he regretted his choice when Mariana propped herself on the arm of the chair and draped her arm across his shoulders. Deborah ended up wedged between a couple of men on the couch, and Jason envied them.

There was a lot of laughter as some of the gifts spoofed Rachel's interests. The football bloopers tape was appreciated by Paul, but everyone knew Rachel hated football. Another gift was a cookbook, and Rachel already had a huge collection.

When Rachel unwrapped a Clint Black video from her brother, however, she crossed the room to give him a hug, allowing him to break out of Mariana's smothering hold.

"Oh, thank you, Jason. I didn't know you knew I liked Clint Black."

"There's something to go with it, but I'll give it to you later," he whispered.

Her eyes sparkled with anticipation, but Jason barely noticed as his attention returned to Deborah.

Rachel invited everyone into the dining room for the buffet and promised to play the football bloopers tape on the big screen television in the den as entertainment while they ate. There was a concerted rush for the food.

Ignoring Mariana behind him, Jason walked over and offered a hand to Deborah. "Need some help up, Deb?"

After a slight hesitation, she took his hand and smiled. "Yes, thank you, Jason. This couch is rather low to the ground." She released his hand as soon as she stood. "Hello, Mariana. That's a nice outfit."

Mariana's hand clasped his arm, and he realized he had

no idea what his date was wearing. Deborah distracted him from that annoying realization.

"Have you both met Joe Swenson? We all went to Texas Christian University together."

Swenson drew Jason's attention from Deborah as he asked him questions about Jason's past experiences. When he turned around, Deborah had gone. Mariana, however, still hung on to his arm.

"Well, shall we go eat? I'm starving," he suggested, sure Deborah had gone on to the buffet. However, she wasn't hovering around the table as everyone else seemed to be.

"I'll see if Rachel needs any help in the kitchen. Joe, could you make sure Mariana gets everything she needs?" he asked, making a friend for life in Joe Swenson.

"Sure. Be glad to."

The kitchen was full of the catering staff, but no Deborah. Jason continued on into the den and persuaded Paul to tell him where to find Deborah.

"I thought I'd give Rachel the rest of her birthday present, too," he added, as incentive.

Paul led him down the hallway to the master bedroom and knocked on the door. "Rachel? Can a couple of guys come in?"

His wife opened the door. "What's the matter? Has the party crashed?"

"Nope. Just a little surprise for you. Open up?"

"Sure." She held the door open wide and Jason discovered Deborah sitting on the edge of the king-sized bed.

"What's the surprise?" Rachel demanded.

Jason forced his gaze away from Deborah and reached in his jacket pocket to bring out the tickets and backstage passes.

Rachel squealed and threw herself into his arms when she realized what he was holding. "Oh, Jason! This is perfect. Thank you so much. How did you know?"

"Deborah told me."

"Oh, this is wonderful! Four tickets? Four! You and Deborah can go with us! What fun!"

Deborah only smiled and edged toward the door.

"How about it, Deborah? Do you like Clint Black?" Jason persisted, unwilling to let her slip away.

"Of course. But right now, I'm going to get some of that wonderful food. I'm starving."

"Me, too. I'll join you." He read the refusal in her eyes, but he ignored it.

"We'd better get back to the party," Paul reminded his wife. "After all, you're the hostess."

They headed back down the hallway. Just as they reached the dining room, however, Deborah stopped. "Oh, I forgot to tell Carol something. I'll be right back." She headed toward the den.

Jason stared after her. She was acting strangely this evening. Avoiding him. That was what he'd intended, of course, Wednesday evening, when he'd reminded her of Mariana. But he wasn't enjoying the results.

In fact, he hadn't enjoyed much of anything since Wednesday night.

"Who's Carol?" he growled.

"An old friend. What did you do to Deb?" Rachel whispered.

He picked up a plate and studied the offerings as if making a major decision. "Nothing."

"Ha! She hasn't spoken to Carol since Randall died. I know because Carol was talking to me before Deborah arrived."

"You'll have to ask Deborah about that," he said calmly, though he hated having his thought confirmed. "I'm not the one who went to talk to Carol."

His gaze lit on Deborah as soon as he entered the den, and he headed toward her. He didn't mind her keeping her distance, but she was being ridiculous about it. Just before he reached her, she stood and exited the other door.

"Jason, I'm over here," Mariana cooed, but he heard the edge in her voice.

"Oh, hi. I didn't see you. Thanks for saving me a place." Like hell. He scowled at his food.

When Deborah came back to the den with a plate with only a few bites of food, she chose a seat on the other side of the room from him and Mariana. At least he could look at her. She couldn't keep him from doing that.

No, but she could drive him insane by talking to Swenson non-stop. When she got up a few minutes later and headed for the dining room again, he gathered his plate.

"What are you doing?" Mariana demanded sharply.

"I'm—I'm going to get a little more brisket. It's terrific."

"You still have some."

"Yeah, but I want more."

"I'll get it for you."

"No, thanks. I don't like to be waited on." He had to tug to free his arm from her clutches, but he didn't give in to her pressure.

When he reached the dining room, he found only his sister. "I thought Deborah came in here."

"She did."

"Where is she now?"

"She left."

"What? Where's she going?" He put his plate down and turned to the front door.

"Jason." Rachel's quiet voice stopped him.

"Yeah?"

"I—I wanted you two to be friends, but I think Deborah needs some space. Don't crowd her."

He ground his teeth in frustration. "I'm not."

"Good. Come on back in the den. I'm going to put on the video you gave me. I want you to watch it with me."

As soon as he'd watched enough of the video to satisfy Rachel, he excused himself and Mariana. It was only ten o'clock, but he'd had enough.

"Well, I'm glad we finally left," Mariana said as he slid behind the wheel. She was already leaning toward his bucket seat, waiting to touch him. "I've been hoping to be alone for the last hour."

"You soon will be. I'll have you home in no time," he said, his mind on Deborah.

There was a cold silence that warned him he'd made a mistake. "What's wrong?"

"I meant the *two* of us alone. Do I have to spell it out for you, Jason? I want you!"

He sighed. No, she didn't have to spell it out for him. She'd been obvious from the beginning. He was the one who was going to have to spell out a few things.

"I'm flattered, Mariana, but I'm afraid I really—that is, you're a very attractive woman, but, as you know, I'm not planning on hanging around Fort Worth much longer. I just don't think it would be fair to start something I couldn't finish."

"That's so honorable of you, Jason, but we could have fun while it lasted," she suggested, slipping her hand inside his jacket to stroke his chest.

"No, I don't think so," he said, removing her hand from him. "I don't operate that way."

"I don't think you operate at all!" she spat at him.

"You're welcome to your opinion," he said and started the car. He ignored her pout. His thoughts were already on Deborah.

Eight

"Deborah, I have another favor to ask."

Jason's husky baritone sent shivers down Deborah's spine and she clutched the telephone receiver more tightly. "What?"

"I need a date for a reception this evening."

It was Sunday afternoon, two days after Rachel's birthday party. Deborah had spent the time assuring herself that she wasn't in love with Jason Bridges. Life without him was just fine. She wasn't about to waste two days of hard work by exposing herself to his brand of attraction so soon.

"Mariana—"

"Mariana isn't speaking to me—and I don't expect her to any time in the near future."

He sounded quite cheerful about their break-up.

"Why?"

"It doesn't matter, does it?" he replied, irritation creeping into his voice. "The end result's the same. I need someone to go with me this evening. Will you?"

Deborah shivered again, fighting the desire to see him. She'd promised herself she'd steer clear of the danger he represented. "No, I'm sorry, but I—I have something planned."

A tense silence followed her weak excuse. Then he demanded, "What?"

She didn't try to avoid answering him. He was too stubborn.

"I'm working."

"Just consider the reception as work, too. I'm your boss, and I need you."

Her acquiescence began to feel inevitable, but she tried again. "Jason, I don't want to go. Call Rachel. She'll know someone else you can invite."

"Deborah, this isn't a date. I can't ask a stranger to accompany me to a reception on a Sunday afternoon. I'll look for someone to take to all these official functions next week, but right now I'm in a bind. I'm asking you, as a friend, to help me out."

She latched onto his words, "as a friend." It gave justification to her desire to see him again. And she *had* decided they could be friends. Of course, she'd intended to avoid him as much as possible, but surely she could spend one evening with him without falling in love with the man.

After all, he was human. He had faults, just like everyone else. Tonight she'd just search for a few of them.

"Deborah?"

"All right. I'll help you out. As a friend."

"Great. I'll pick you up at five-thirty."

"What do I wear? Who's the reception for?" she asked quickly.

"It's dressy. We're welcoming an investment group from France."

A few hours later, in the ballroom of one of Fort Worth's most prestigious hotels, Deborah was busy compiling her woefully short list of Jason's faults. So far, the only notation was his possessiveness. Even as a friend, he was possessive. When one of the Frenchmen got too close to her, Jason removed Deborah from the man's grasp, and his French was quite good enough to convey his objections.

Deborah was a little unclear about whether that was a shortcoming, especially since she didn't like the Frenchman touching her anymore than Jason did, but she was desperate for *something* to put on her list.

Already she'd listed the scar on his cheek. She'd intended to ask him how he'd received it. Her fascination with it made it a doubtful candidate for her list also.

"I can't wait to get out of here," Jason muttered under his breath as he leaned toward her, smiling at the others in his group at the same time.

Aha! He was two-faced! Well, sort of. And she couldn't help agreeing with him.

A young woman joined their group and immediately attached herself to Jason. That was the worst thing she had against him, Deborah decided. He was extremely attractive to the opposite sex. Including herself. A major fault.

Of course, the fact that he wasn't encouraging the young woman was in his favor. Since she was concentrating on his imperfections, Deborah was unprepared when his arm went around her shoulders.

"Help me out here, before this female piranha has me for dinner." His whisper tickled her ear. In a normal tone of voice, he continued, "Sweetheart, have you met Eunice Cary?"

"No, I don't believe I have. I'm Deborah Townsend." She extended her hand to the young woman, forcing her to release Jason's arm with at least one hand.

Eunice's greeting was decidedly cooler to Deborah, particularly as Jason withdrew the two of them from the group almost simultaneously, leaving Miss Cary with a frustrated look on her face.

"Let's find the mayor and make our excuses," Jason suggested, already searching the crowd.

He made decisions without waiting for her agreement. That had to be a huge fault. Even if she agreed with him. After all, she was an independent woman. Then why was she doing exactly as he said, she asked herself.

"Shouldn't we stay until it's over?" she suggested, and even to her ears her words sounded feeble.

He turned and stared down at her in mock horror. "You must be running a fever. Otherwise you'd never make such an inane suggestion."

Another fault. He was a tease. Not such a terrible flaw since it tempted her to smile, but still a candidate for her list. "Okay, I was just trying to be helpful."

"You've been terrific tonight." His arm tightened around her shoulder, pressing her against him. "I can't tell you what a relief it's been."

"What do you mean?" she asked breathlessly. No fault could be found with him physically, she decided. Unless it was the fact that he was too overpowering. Maybe she was just too susceptible. She hadn't thought so until Jason Bridges walked into her office only a couple of weeks ago.

"Mariana couldn't be relied on to, uh, behave."

"At a formal reception?" Her eyebrows soared.

"Anywhere," was his terse reply.

"My, you must've led an exciting life." Her teasing brought a grin to his lips that caused her heartbeat to increase.

"Yeah, and I'm too old for such shenanigans."

"Ah. No wonder you want to leave early. You need a glass of warm milk and an early bedtime." The look of pure innocence she shot him brought more of a response than she'd intended as he quickly kissed her.

She blinked several times, trying to catch her breath, unsure what to say. The mayor saved her.

"Jason, Deborah, you're not leaving already?" His booming voice pierced Deborah's haze.

Jason seemed unaffected as he turned to greet the mayor. "Why, yes, Mayor, we have another party to attend after this one, so we'll have to leave early. But it was a wonderful reception. I think we made a hit with the French invasion."

Jason took his arm from around Deborah, leaving her strangely chilled, while he shook the mayor's hand.

"I know this little lady did," the mayor said, indicating Deborah. "They were impressed with your sense of fashion. Seems they expected everyone to be in jeans and boots, even at a formal reception." He chuckled over the image Fort Worth and Texas had around the world.

"I'm glad I held up Fort Worth's fashion reputation, Mayor," Deborah said, pleased with her faux-Chanel navy suit trimmed with white. "But I'm sure your wife could've managed it all by herself. She looks beautiful this evening."

"I'll tell her you said so, Deborah. And by the way, it's good to see you back out in society again. We've missed you."

Deborah only nodded with a stiff smile as Jason urged her to the door. When they stepped outside, she drew a deep breath of cleansing night air, crisply cool after a warm day.

"You're really good at these social things, aren't you?" Jason asked as he drew her arm through his.

"I've attended a great many receptions in the past."

"So has Mariana, but she never showed any expertise. I think that's because she found any subject but herself boring."

"Jason! That's not a gentlemanly thing to say."

"I know. I'm not always a gentleman."

Ah. A self-admitted fault. But was it less of a fault because he admitted it? Deborah couldn't decide. She only knew she needed to find more flaws if she intended to use her list as protection against his charm.

He helped her into his car, a deep green Jaguar. After only a few blocks of contemplating his imperfections and their amazing attractiveness, she realized they weren't heading in the direction of her house. "Where are we going?"

"I'm taking you to dinner. And not a French restaurant. I've about had it with French accents this evening."

"But Jason, I really need—"

"To eat something. You deserve dinner after the wonderful job you did."

"I didn't really do anything," she protested.

He stopped the car in front of an elegant restaurant. "I appreciate your modesty, Deborah, but, believe me, you handled the entire evening beautifully. Dinner's the least I can do."

Deborah gave up the fight. Perhaps it was for the best. The last time they'd dined together, he'd thrown Mariana in her face when it was over. Maybe he'd reveal his worst faults over the meal. Or offend her in some way. Or even abandon her. She could only pray.

In spite of her thoughts, dinner was delightful. Jason could spin tales with the best of them, and he set out to amuse her. Time flew by. She even asked about the scar on his brow. Though he laughed off the danger, fear squeezed Deborah's heart as he talked about the civil war in a far off country.

The drive to her home was almost totally silent, a silence that was even more telling to Deborah than their talk over dinner. She was content to be beside him, to watch his strong hands on the wheel, to exchange warm glances.

He walked her to her door. Fearful that he might try a goodnight kiss, Deborah was reluctant to face him. Instead, he raised a hand and allowed one knuckle to caress her flushed cheek.

"Thanks, Deb, for helping me out. I'll be glad when I can go back to being a reporter and won't have to attend these blasted receptions every other night."

"You're welcome," she said hastily and unlocked her door. "Goodnight," she called over her shoulder and slipped inside to lean against the closed door.

Finally she had a major fault to add to her list. The most important fault of all. The fault that made it impossible to love Jason Bridges.

He was going to leave.
She only hoped she hadn't made her list in vain.

Jason found himself whistling as he drove back to his
apartment. The reception hadn't been nearly as boring as
he'd expected it to be. Deborah's company had added to the
evening.

She was certainly a natural at social gatherings, greeting
people with sincerity, warmth, drawing them into a conversation. Too bad he couldn't just hire her to attend the parties
and receptions with him.

His lips stretched into a wry grin. Instead, he'd have to
find another lady willing to date him with no strings attached, and Deborah would have to find someone—*willing
to do the same.*

Of course! She was reluctant to date again. He supposed
she didn't want to get involved with anyone because she
still loved her husband. He could be wrong. It could be that
she was just in a rut, or afraid to try dating again. Or something.

But they had the same problem. Neither of them wanted
to lead anyone into believing they might be serious about
a relationship. Yet both of them, for different reasons,
needed to date.

How simple!

Now, all he had to do was convince Deborah his plan
would solve both their problems.

Suddenly, life in Fort Worth, Texas, looked as exciting as
any overseas assignment he'd ever had.

The next morning came too early for Deborah. Monday
was never her favorite day, but sleep had proved elusive
last night. Since she didn't punch a time clock, she'd turned
over and slept later than usual.

Though she still felt the remnants of her disturbed night, when she reached the office, one look at the note on her desk at work washed the lassitude from her body.

She didn't want to call Jason. Could she pretend she never got the message? Would he forget he'd called? Of course not. Jason would simply call again if she didn't contact him. With a sigh, she picked up the phone.

"Jason? I just got in and found a message to call you."

"It's about time. The rest of us have been here for hours." She could hear the warm, teasing note in his voice but it didn't make her happy.

"And?"

"A little snippy this morning, aren't we?" When she didn't answer, he continued, "I just wanted to check with you about lunch."

"What about lunch?"

"I want to take you out to lunch. I have a new plan to talk over." His enthusiasm made her leery.

"About what?"

"I don't want to tell you over the phone. I'll be ready to go in about an hour. Is that all right with you?"

"I really think it would be better if we had a meeting here in the office instead of over lunch," she said, trying to keep her voice cool and firm.

"Nope. In about an hour." Without waiting for a reply, he hung up.

"That man is going to drive me crazy," Deborah muttered as she replaced the receiver. Did he always have to get his way?

Her hand was still resting on the telephone when it rang, causing her to jump at least several inches. She stared at it, trying to decide if Jason was calling her again. Finally, she lifted the receiver.

"Hello?"

"Deborah, Deborah, she said yes!"

"Manny? Oh, that's wonderful. I thought she would. How

could anyone turn down a great guy like you? I'm so happy for both of you."

"I'm the one who's lucky. And I owe it all to you, Deborah. If it hadn't been for you encouraging me, explaining to me how Elizabeth felt, I never would've kept on."

"I'm glad you did. And I didn't really know exactly how Elizabeth felt. I could only guess because I'm a widow, too. But I'm glad everything worked out." She sighed with happiness.

"Elizabeth wants to talk to you."

He must've handed the phone to his future bride because the next voice Deborah heard was Elizabeth's.

"Deborah, we want you to come to the wedding," Elizabeth's soft voice pleaded, as if she feared Deborah might turn down her invitation.

"Of course I'll come to the wedding. Just tell me when and you couldn't keep me away."

"Well, dear, we want you to be *in* the wedding. You know I have no children, and—and I wondered if you'd be my maid of honor."

Deborah was overwhelmed. She'd been coaching Manny in his courtship of Elizabeth for almost a year. First they'd corresponded after he'd written a letter to her column. Then he'd called her at the office when he'd panicked over the next step. Eventually, she'd talked to Elizabeth also. The three of them had become fast friends. But she'd never expected Elizabeth to ask her to stand up with her.

"But Elizabeth, don't you have friends who would expect to be asked?"

"Without you, Deborah, I never would've had the courage to accept, and Manny says he'd never have asked. And we're so happy!"

Her voice was filled with joy and contentment, with sharing. Deborah fought the envy that crept up and answered even more warmly. "Of course I'll be in your wedding, Elizabeth, if that's what you and Manny want."

"Oh, it is, dear. Now, are you free next Sunday afternoon?"

Assuming they were going to celebrate their engagement with a party, or perhaps even have a shower, Deborah grinned. How sweet! "Yes, I believe I am."

"Good. We've planned the ceremony for one o'clock, with a buffet luncheon afterwards. I'd like you to wear something pink, if you have it. Not floor length, of course. I'm going to wear a pale pink tea-length dress. If yours is a little darker, I think that would be charming."

"You're—you're getting *married* next Sunday?"

"Why, yes, dear, that's what we've been talking about, isn't it?"

"But I thought——"

"We thought about waiting, but we really couldn't see the sense in that. Neither of us is getting any younger."

"You're right, there's no reason to wait. Where is this grand event taking place?"

"In my backyard. The roses are just starting to bloom."

After a few more details, Deborah hung up the phone, a satisfied smile on her face. She couldn't be happier for the couple. They were perfect for each other, erasing the loneliness that had enveloped the two of them.

Just like the loneliness that enveloped her. Perhaps her talks with Manny and eventually Elizabeth had helped her through the grieving process, also. She only knew how much she wished them well.

When Jason arrived at her office for lunch, Deborah was still thinking about Manny and Elizabeth, feeling happier than she had in months. From Manny's last letter, the one she'd been reading that had piqued Jason's interest, she'd hoped he would propose soon. She hadn't realized it would be this soon.

"Glad to see you're looking forward to lunch."

Deborah's hands jerked, almost tearing the paper she was holding. "You surprised me. Is it lunchtime already?"

"Ah. That wasn't anticipation I saw on your face?"

"I was working. Are you sure you don't want to have our talk here? Then you could have lunch with—with the mayor or someone."

He sauntered into her cubicle and placed his strong, capable hands on her desk and leaned forward. Deborah stared up into his hazel eyes and pressed against the back of her chair.

"Do you realize you always say no to any invitation I offer? You could deflate my ego, if you're not careful."

The thought of the self-confident male in front of her stripped to a whimpering stub of a man was so ridiculous that Deborah laughed, then said, "Right." She hoped he heard the sarcasm she intended.

"I'm a very sensitive person."

She shook her head even as she stood, hoping he'd retreat slightly. Close proximity with Jason Bridges wasn't good for her blood pressure. "Let's get this lunch meeting over with. I have a lot of letters to read."

"Your enthusiasm for my company is overwhelming," he assured her, taking her arm to escort her to lunch.

"Jason, I'm not going to run away. You don't have to hold onto me."

"My mother taught me to be a gentleman. Do you expect me to let her down just because you're so fussy?" His self-righteous expression was so patently false, she considered arguing with him. Then she shrugged her shoulders. It didn't seem worth the effort. Not when he was going to win anyway.

He took her to a nearby four-star hotel famous for its dining room. Scattered palm trees and restful blues and greens gave it a calm, quiet atmosphere, and the tables were well-spaced, lending an air of privacy. Deborah wondered if the imaginary firing they'd discussed at their first lunch was taking place today. Why else would he bring her here?

"So what's your new plan?" she asked after the Maitre d'

had pulled back her chair and then left them with large, leather-bound menus.

Jason looked mildly surprised. "You already know what you're going to order? I haven't even had a chance to look at it yet. What's good?"

"I don't want to discuss food," she said, almost surprising herself with the intensity of her voice. "I want to know if you brought me here to fire me."

Jason studied her before slowly shaking his head no. "I don't know where you get this anxiety about me firing you, Deborah, but that's not what I have in mind at all." He pointedly looked at his menu. "I think I'll have the Fettucine Alfredo. How about you?"

"Fine," she said through gritted teeth. "I'll have the same."

He signaled to the waiter and gave their order. The waiter collected the menus and faded away. Deborah leaned forward. *"Now* will you tell me your plan?"

"Of course. I'll be happy to. I don't know why I didn't come up with it sooner, but I think you'll be pleased."

She rolled her eyes. If he didn't quit stalling, she'd choke him. "What is it?"

"We're going to start dating each other."

Nine

Deborah was stunned by Jason's words. Though he continued to talk, she could only see his mouth move. Somehow, her brain had ceased to function.

"Deborah?"

Her name snapped her from her daze and she pulled herself together.

"Are you all right?"

"Yes, thank you, Jason. I think the heat got to me," she suggested with a weak smile. Never mind that it was a balmy seventy degrees outside and the hotel was climate controlled. It was the only excuse she could come up with. "Could I have some iced tea to drink?"

While Jason was catching the waiter's eye, Deborah tried to organize her thoughts. Date each other? Was the man out of his mind? That was the last thing she wanted to do. But she'd have to be very careful. Already she'd put herself at risk by her reaction to his words.

"Are you sure you're all right? You went kind of pale," Jason said as he watched the waiter set a frosted glass of iced tea in front of her.

"Oh, yes, I'm fine. I didn't want to admit it, but I'm afraid I woke up late and didn't eat breakfast. That always makes me a little lightheaded. I'll feel much better when I've eaten." *And when I stop rattling on.* Jason was going to think she was a blooming idiot at this rate.

"I'll get you some crackers." Even as he started to wave to their waiter again, Deborah stopped him.

"Oh, no, that's not necessary. I wouldn't want to spoil my appetite." She chewed on her bottom lip, grateful when he didn't respond to her ridiculous statement. The only good thing to come from her bizarre behavior was that Jason seemed to have forgotten his plan.

He continued to stare, his eyes never leaving her face, making her more and more nervous. She reached for the glass of tea and sipped the cold liquid. Anything to distract him.

His voice a soothing baritone, he launched into an amusing story about his search for an iced drink in the Middle East. Even though Deborah realized he was trying to entertain her, to set her at ease, he did just that. She could never resist his anecdotes.

By the time he finished, their food arrived. Deborah discovered she really was hungry, almost convinced that she'd told the truth about not eating breakfast. She even almost convinced herself that Jason hadn't mentioned anything disturbing earlier.

Almost.

Until they finished eating.

"Feeling better?"

"Oh, yes, much. That was a delicious meal."

"Good. Then we can talk about my plan."

She struggled to maintain a passive expression on her face. It was difficult with her heart thumping like a drum. "I assumed you were teasing."

Frowning, he stared at her. "Why would I do that?"

Shrugging her shoulders, she said nothing.

"I'm not teasing. It will solve both our problems."

The man was insane! Their dating would create more problems than a forty day flood. "I didn't know I had a problem." Other than him, of course.

"Sure you do. We both do. That's when I realized how easily we could solve them."

He looked quite pleased with himself, and Deborah wanted to kick him in the shin. "Oh?"

"I assume you don't want to date because of your feelings for your husband."

A surge of guilt shot through Deborah. Her fears had nothing to do with Randall. Not because she didn't still love him. She always would. But she'd also discovered she could fall in love again. No, her qualms were all centered in the confident male across from her.

Jason didn't notice her reaction. He continued with his explanation. "I don't want to date because I'm only here temporarily. Besides, I don't want a woman to think I have anything permanent in mind. So, if we date each other, neither of us will expect anything, but we'll both be solving our problem. Brilliant, isn't it?"

"Absolutely," she said, barely breathing, before bending to pick up her purse from the floor.

"So we're agreed?" he asked with an easy smile.

"No. We're not. And I have to get back to the office."

She stood and walked from the restaurant, ignoring his call. Since they'd walked the two blocks to the hotel, Deborah wasn't surprised when Jason caught up with her after paying the bill. But at least she'd had a few minutes alone.

A few minutes to realize she was trapped.

"What's the matter, Deborah?" he demanded, a frown on his brow, as he grabbed her arm and stopped her. "There's nothing that urgent waiting for you at the office."

"No. I just don't think your plan is necessary."

"You mean you've already found someone to date?"

"No! I mean—I mean, I don't think it's necessary," she finished lamely.

"Well, I do. You need an escort. I clearly need someone to take to all these damned parties and receptions I keep getting invited to. Otherwise, every mother in the city would start matchmaking."

Deborah stood with her head bowed, letting the inevitable roll over her. Why did it always come to her being cornered, giving in, to this man? But she was trapped because he was right. Their situations made sense put together. And if she protested too much, he might realize the truth.

She'd fallen in love with Jason Bridges.

Gathering every ounce of courage she had, she raised her head, the best smile she could summon pasted to her lips. "And we'd just be friends? Helping each other out?"

"Of course. That's the beauty of the plan. We each get something out of it. You get the needed experience for the column, and I get a beautiful companion whose social skills are excellent."

He grinned, his lips so near hers, his hazel eyes sparkling with shared laughter, his silky hair blown by the spring breeze. Darn. Why couldn't he have been repulsive? she wondered.

Hoping to end her torture, she stuck out her hand. "Then I guess you've got a partner."

Almost as soon as he touched her hand, she withdrew and swung around to continue their walk to the office.

Jason stared after her, wondering what was wrong when she'd just agreed with him. Somehow he knew something was wrong.

He caught up with her, again taking her arm in his. "I'll have Brenda type up a list of all the upcoming social events, so you'll be able to plan ahead." Her arm was trembling and he ducked his head to look at her.

"Are you sure you're feeling all right? Maybe you should go home and rest this afternoon."

"I'm fine," she assured him, but her smile never reached her eyes. "I need to read the letters we received today. With any luck, I'll finish my column early this week so I can concentrate on my wardrobe. It's going to need some updating if I'm going to be accompanying the Editor-in-Chief."

There was a teasing note in her voice that eased his concern. But he hadn't thought about her having to buy any clothes. "I'll be glad to pick up the bill for—"

"No!" Her reply was sharp, but before he could argue with her, she continued, "No, thank you. That's not necessary. Now that I'm emerging from my self-imposed retirement, I'll need the clothes for other things . . . after you're gone."

"Oh, right." They walked on in silence. He didn't like the thought of her going out after he'd left. Of course, he didn't want her retreating again. But what if she chose the wrong man, someone who might hurt her? He'd have to look around for a nice guy to step into his shoes when the time came to leave.

Such an altruistic thought relieved his worries.

When the list was delivered to her desk by the office boy several hours later, Deborah was astounded at the number of social engagements listed, including the Charity Ball in two weeks. Almost every evening was filled, as well as all weekend. Weekend! She remembered her promise to Elizabeth and Manny.

Picking up the phone, she dialed Jason's secretary. "Brenda? Thanks for the list, but I won't be available next Sunday."

"Oh? Well, Mr. Bridges is in. Would you like to talk to him?"

"No! No, just make a note for him. It's not important enough to interrupt his work. I'm sure it won't matter to him." He could take Rachel, or go alone, or drop dead, as far as she was concerned. Even as she hung up the phone, she knew she hadn't meant such a thing. But the man was driving her crazy.

She had had no idea her entire life would be taken over by Jason when she'd agreed to accompany him. Didn't the man ever say no? With a schedule like this, no wonder he wanted to get away. Covering a small rebellion would look simple in comparison.

She chuckled at her thoughts as she picked up another letter. It was time to concentrate on her job instead of her employer.

"Why can't you go with me Sunday?"

Staring at the masculine temptation leaning against her door, Deborah wondered if he was a genie, popping out of a bottle every time she thought of him. That was the only way to explain his constant appearances.

"I already have plans. You can take Rachel, or—or go alone."

He sauntered closer to her desk, and Deborah felt her blood pressure soar. She returned her gaze to the letter in her hand.

"But you agreed to go with me."

"Jason, when I agreed, I assumed you were talking about a couple of times a week. Mick Jagger might be able to party every night, but I'm not sure I can," she exclaimed in exasperation. "Besides, I only said I couldn't go with you Sunday, not any other time."

"Okay, okay," he agreed irritably and settled down into the chair in front of her desk.

Was he going to stay? Didn't the man have work to do?

"So, will you be busy all day Sunday?"

Her head snapped up. Did he think he owned her? "No."

When she said nothing else, he added, "Because the reception is two to four. Maybe you could get away for those two hours."

"Jason, you're going to a library dedication, not your senior prom. It won't matter if you go alone." She almost grinned at the look on his face. It felt good to have the upper hand for once. He clearly wanted to know her plans, and she was just as determined not to tell him.

She wasn't sure he'd approve anyway. She shouldn't have gotten so closely involved in Elizabeth and Manny's romance. Mr. Campbell, her previous editor, had warned her about doing so.

"True. But an old friend asked me out to dinner Sunday evening, with his wife, of course, and I accepted for both of us."

Deborah raised her eyebrows. "Don't you think you should've checked with me first? Or have we returned to the days of slavery?"

He confounded her by apologizing at once. "You're right. I'm sorry. He called just after we got back from lunch and I was so relieved that I had that problem solved, I didn't even think about checking with you. But I promise I'll do so from now on."

His sincere tone and warm gaze had Deborah swallowing and blinking several times. "I—I suppose I could get free for dinner, if it's important."

He smiled and Deborah decided he'd probably learned its potency in the cradle. "Thanks, Deb, I'd appreciate it."

When he said nothing else, just smiling at her, not moving, she finally asked, "Is there anything else?"

"I was just wondering when you'd be free Sunday. I can make the dinner late if I need to."

His friendly warmth and casual air almost fooled her before she realized he was probing again. "Oh, I don't think you mentioned a time."

"Six o'clock?"

"Really? That seems early for a dinner invitation, but I think I'll be home by then." She thought she'd be home by three, but she was determined not to tell him. Perhaps she was being petty, but he always seemed to win the war. She could at least win this one battle.

Smiling sweetly, she picked up a letter to read. He took the hint and stood.

"Good. That's good. I'll pick you up at—at five-thirty?"

"I'll be ready. Shall I dress casual or—"

"Casual. I refuse to spend the evening in a suit, if I have to dress up for the library thing." He wandered to the door, seemingly not in a hurry to leave. "Everything else on the list okay?"

"I think so, though occasionally something may come up. I didn't realize you led such an active social life."

"It'll settle down after a while. Once the novelty wears off."

"Or you leave."

He frowned at her. "I'll be around for a while."

"Oh, yes, of course." He'd be around for a while. Just long enough to thoroughly ensnare her in his charm, his warmth, his—heart. And then he'd go away.

Two days later Jason was looking over the latest circulation figures when his secretary knocked on his door.

"Mr. Bridges, there's a gentleman here to see you. He says his name is Emanuel Lipscher, and his business is personal, concerning an employee."

Without looking up, Jason asked, "Did you refer him to Personnel?"

"I tried, but he said he wanted *you* to know how much one of our employees had helped him." She moved closer to the desk and lowered her voice. "He's a really sweet, older gentleman, and I just couldn't turn him away."

Jason looked up in surprise. Normally, Brenda was ferocious when protecting his work time. Smiling, he nodded his head. "Okay, show him in. But if I buzz you, come interrupt us and tell me I have a long distance call."

He put aside his papers and prepared to do five minutes of public relations work with Mr. Lipscher.

The man entering his office was in his sixties, Jason decided, though in good shape. He was dressed in a navy suit, his silver hair styled, and a beaming smile on his face. No wonder Brenda hadn't been able to resist him.

Jason stood and offered his hand. "Good morning, Mr. Lipscher. I understand you have some compliments for one of our employees? Please, be seated."

"Yes, sir, Mr. Bridges, I have. One of your employees has changed my life. She's gone out of her way for me, and she's become a good friend."

Already, Jason's thoughts were drifting back to those critical numbers, sure that Mr. Lipscher must live next door to one of the nice ladies from Classifieds who'd been romancing him. His next words only confirmed Jason's thoughts.

"I'm being married this Sunday, and I thought you should know that it wouldn't be happening without her."

"Congratulations. Does this mean I'll be losing an employee?"

The gentleman frowned at him. "Why would you lose an employee?"

"If you're marrying her, she might decide to stay home."

"Oh, I'm not marrying Deborah. I'm marrying Elizabeth."

Jason's thoughts skidded to a halt. He looked at Mr. Lipscher more closely. "Deborah? The employee you're talking about is Deborah Townsend?"

"Why, yes. Didn't I mention that? Sorry, I thought you'd know. I wrote to Deborah almost a year ago for advice because I—" he paused, his cheeks red, "I fell in love with Elizabeth and I didn't know how to tell her."

"I see."

"I was the oldest child of a large family. When my father died, I took over for him. Got a job, helped Ma raise the rest of them. By the time the youngest had finished school,

I was almost forty." He shrugged his shoulders. "It seemed life had passed me by. I'm kind of shy," he confessed.

"With women, most of us are," Jason agreed, a twinkle in his eye.

"Anyway, I didn't have much experience. And Elizabeth is a widow. She was afraid to, you know, offer any encouragement. If it hadn't been for Deborah, I would of never gotten the courage."

"I'm happy for you, Mr. Lipscher. In fact," he paused to think about the idea that had just struck him, "in fact, I'd like to do a feature story on what happened. It would help Deborah. Sort of unpaid advertising for her column. Would you and Elizabeth mind?"

"We would do anything for Deborah," the man eagerly assured him.

"When did you say the wedding will be?"

"This Sunday afternoon. Deborah is going to be Elizabeth's Maid of Honor."

Jason paused imperceptibly before reaching for the phone. This Sunday? That's why Deborah couldn't accompany him to the library dedication. They'd gone to a reception last night and he'd hinted again about what she had planned for Sunday. Not that it mattered. It was just that he felt responsible for her. He was afraid she might fall for the wrong kind of guy.

"Have you and Elizabeth hired a photographer for the wedding?" he asked before he dialed.

"No. A friend was just going to take a few pictures."

"Our staff photographer will take pictures for you and we'll put them in an album afterwards."

Manny beamed at him. "That's wonderful. Elizabeth will be so pleased."

"Where are you going for your honeymoon?" Jason's mind was working at a fast clip. This situation was a P. R. goldmine. The man just shrugged his shoulders.

"I'd planned for a hotel room Sunday evening, but I

wasn't sure Elizabeth wanted anything more. We're both older, you know."

Grinning, Jason winked at him. "I think you and Elizabeth deserve a little more than that. Let me see what I can do."

He picked up the phone, giving brief instructions to the photographer who answered, ordering him to his office. Then he called the travel editor and asked her to come also. Hanging up the phone, he looked at his visitor again.

"Did you only have the one letter to Deborah?"

"Oh, no. I wrote back, after she gave me such good advice. We've been corresponding pretty regularly ever since. Sometimes we talk on the phone. But I'm more comfortable putting my thoughts on paper."

Ah. The call she'd said was personal. Could it have been one of Mr. Lipscher's, instead of a boyfriend? Jason was finding this conversation very satisfying.

"Let me get a feature writer up here to do a story on you and Elizabeth. Why don't you go to my secretary's desk and use her phone to call Elizabeth and be sure this is all right with her. The reporter might want to visit with the two of you today or tomorrow, when it's convenient."

"Of course. Anything for Deborah."

Jason escorted the man to Brenda's desk and started to leave, before remembering something else. "Oh, by the way, Mr. Lipscher, would it upset you and your bride if I attended the wedding? I don't want to throw off the numbers any."

"Why no, Mr. Bridges. We'd love to have you."

"Great. I'll escort Deborah."

Manny looked at him with a frown. "You know Deborah well?"

"Oh, yes. We're good friends." Jason didn't elaborate. After all, he wasn't sure she'd be speaking to him when she found out what he was doing.

After a talk with the travel editor and the feature writer and photographer, Jason decided he'd better have a talk with

Deborah. He strolled down to her office, anticipating her reaction.

"Deb, what time shall I pick you up Sunday?" he asked, leaning, as usual, against the doorjamb.

She'd been working at her computer and looked at him, still thinking about her writing. "What?"

He repeated his questions and she stared at him.

"We agreed on five-thirty," she reminded him impatiently, running a hand through her blond hair. He stuck his hands in his pockets before he could give into the temptation to do the same thing.

"I don't think that will be early enough for the wedding, will it?" He tried to keep the smile from his face. He knew they'd been playing a cat and mouse game, though he wasn't sure why. Having given up finding out what he wanted to know, it was particularly pleasing to have it dumped in his lap.

Now he had her full attention.

"What are you talking about?"

"Mr. Lipscher and Elizabeth's wedding."

"You know them?"

"Well, I've met the gentleman. I'm only using Elizabeth's first name because he neglected to tell me her last name."

"Why have you talked to Manny?"

"He came to my office to sing your praises."

"And you finagled an invitation to their wedding?" Deborah demanded, irritation on her beautiful face.

"A lot more than that, Deborah, my dear. A lot more than that."

Ten

Deborah slowly stood, never taking her gaze from the aggravating man. "Jason, what do you mean?"

"Nothing much."

His grin didn't reassure her. She rounded the desk. "It wasn't Manny's fault. Don't—don't mess up their wedding."

Jason frowned, straightening from his normal slouch against her doorjamb. "What do you take me for, Deb? The Grinch? Why would I do that?"

Her eyes searched for some sign of his intent. "Because I know you don't like weddings—marriage. And I know I shouldn't have gotten so involved. But Manny and Elizabeth didn't do anything wrong. I don't want this special moment ruined for them." She fought back the tears that filled her eyes. Somehow, Manny and Elizabeth's happiness meant a great deal to her.

Jason's mouth tightened in anger. "Oh, I've really messed things up for them. We're providing photographs of the wedding, a free honeymoon to the Caribbean and a beautiful wedding cake. Let's see . . . what else can I do to ruin their lives?"

"You've done all that? Why?" Deborah was somewhat relieved but still guarded. "You don't believe in marriage."

"Don't be ridiculous. Just because marriage isn't for me doesn't mean I'm against it for other people."

"Oh." She swallowed and tentatively reached out a hand

to touch his arm in apology. "I didn't mean to imply that you would be cruel. I just—Manny and Elizabeth are special. They've both been alone and now they're so happy to have found each other."

"Apology accepted," he muttered. Then, without any warning, he pulled Deborah into his arms. "Don't cry, Deb. We're going to make their wedding quite an event."

Pressed against his broad chest, warm arms enveloping her, his scent a combination of cologne, fresh air, and just plain Jason, Deborah struggled to regain her composure. It was an uphill battle, particularly against her own body, which pleaded to remain pressed against his.

Panicked over the desire that filled her, Deborah pushed away from him. "That's wonderful," she mumbled and backed toward her desk.

"Want to come up and talk to the soon-to-be newlyweds, to be sure? Elizabeth's on her way over and Manny's talking to a feature writer now."

"But why? Neither of them wanted publicity. Why would they seek out an interview?" Suddenly Deborah was questioning the unusual events Jason spoke of.

"Manny wanted to be sure you get credit for being such a good friend."

Outraged, she stared at Jason. "You're using him, aren't you? For publicity! Jason, how could you? You *are* going to spoil their wedding!"

"Why do I feel like I'm on a roller coaster ride? Would you stop attacking me? Manny has no problem with what we're doing. Why do you?"

His reasonable voice didn't calm Deborah. She pushed past him. "I'm going to speak to Manny."

"That's what I suggested," he called, turning to follow her.

Deborah didn't wait for him. She sped down the hall to the stairs and dashed up two floors, Jason right behind her.

"Where is he?" she asked as they topped the stairs.

"They were in my secretary's office."

She rushed into Brenda's domain and immediately spotted Manny's silver hair. "Manny? I need to talk to you."

"Deborah! Has Mr. Bridges told you everything? Isn't he wonderful?"

Deborah glared at the man beside her, a triumphant smile on his face. "We'll see. Come in here," she said, gesturing toward Jason's office. "I'm sure Mr. Bridges will allow us a few minutes alone in his office."

Jason nodded, still grinning, and the gray-haired man and Deborah disappeared into the other room, closing the door behind them. She was acting like a hen with one chick, Jason decided. Too bad she didn't have children. Deborah Townsend would make a terrific mother.

He frowned. The thought of Deborah with children gave him pause. Not that he wouldn't have been happy for her to have children. He would, of course. Dismissing such confusing thoughts, he turned at the sound of someone behind him. A patrician lady, her light brown hair threaded with silver, stood hesitantly in the doorway.

"Elizabeth?" he guessed.

Startled, she stared at him. "Why, yes. I wasn't sure I'd found the right office. Is Manny . . . Mr. Emanuel Lipscher here?"

"Yes, he is, but—he's in conference right now. Why don't we sit down and let me explain what's going on." He introduced his secretary and Clare, the reporter who'd been interviewing Manny. Then he launched into an explanation.

"I agree with Manny," Elizabeth said after he'd finished. "We owe Deborah everything. But will a lot of people come to the wedding? Strangers?"

"No, of course not. In fact, I'm the only change in the guest list, Elizabeth, if you don't mind, except for the photographer and Clare. I'm going to escort Deborah."

A beaming smile broke across Elizabeth's face. "Oh, I'm so glad. She's such a wonderful person. I don't want her to be lonely either."

The room suddenly seemed smaller, with three pairs of female eyes on him, and Jason cleared his throat. "We're just friends, you know. I mean, she and my sister went to school together."

Elizabeth arched one delicate brow. "I see. Well, she's certainly a lovely person."

"Uh, yeah." He was relieved when the door opened behind him.

"Elizabeth!" Manny rushed toward his fiancee as if he hadn't seen her in months. The two embraced as Elizabeth stood. Wrapped in each other's arms, they whispered their greetings. Jason watched them, surprised when something akin to envy entered his head.

He turned to look at Deborah and found her lost in the tender scene before them. She'd never looked more beautiful.

"Elizabeth says you've already explained everything, Mr. Bridges," Manny said, smiling at him. "So, I guess we're ready to start her part of the interview."

"Elizabeth, are you sure you want to do this? I can manage without the publicity," Deborah assured the woman.

"I don't mind the interview, Deborah. But I'm not sure anyone will be interested in it." She smiled lovingly up at Manny. "After all, we're just two old people who—who happened to find each other."

Manny cupped her cheek with his weathered palm. "And we'll never be apart again."

Jason found it difficult to speak. He cleared his throat. "I think everyone is interested in a happy ending, Elizabeth. We have to print so much bad news these days. Your story will bring a smile to our readers' faces."

"Then I'm ready. I have so much happiness, I'm willing to share."

"Great. Clare," he said to the reporter, "why don't you take the two of them into the conference room next door and finish your interview."

The three people left the office and Brenda sighed. "What a lovely couple."

"Yes, they are," Deborah agreed fervently.

"No wonder you got involved," Jason commented, still staring at the door where they'd disappeared.

Deborah stiffened beside him. "I know I shouldn't have gotten so close to them, but—"

"I wasn't criticizing. You haven't done anything wrong. In fact, because of you, we're going to have a feature story that will bring a lot of happiness." He gestured to his secretary. "Look at Brenda. She hasn't stopped smiling."

"Well, they're so—so tender with each other. It makes you want to hug someone," Brenda said.

Jason carefully avoided looking at Deborah after one glance at her red cheeks. But their earlier embrace filled his head. He'd meant it to console Deborah. Instead, he'd made it impossible to stand beside her without touching her. His fingers hungered to stroke her warm skin.

"I'd better get back to my office," Deborah said in a rush, hurrying over to the door. "I—I need to finish my column."

"Why don't you add a note to Manny and Elizabeth at the end of the column, sort of a wish for their future. It will draw attention to their story which will be in Saturday's edition."

She gave a jerky nod and turned to leave.

"Don't forget that banquet tonight. I'll pick you up at seven."

She didn't respond.

As the speaker droned on, Deborah thought about the column she'd turned in that afternoon. She'd added a short paragraph about Manny and Elizabeth. After thinking about it, she was no longer angry that Jason was promoting their wedding. The couple seemed pleased about it, and he was right. A lot of people would enjoy, second-hand, their happiness.

Second-hand was the closest some people could come to happiness.

"And as our guest this evening, allow me to introduce Mr. Jason Bridges, Editor-in-Chief of the *Fort Worth Daily.*" The speaker's words caught Deborah's attention.

She and Jason were attending a Project Literacy banquet, a cause she could willingly support. She watched as her escort stood and walked to the microphone. He looked so handsome, so intelligent, so . . . sexy. There was no other way to describe him.

Sighing, she tried to concentrate on his words.

"As a toddler, I remember listening to my mother as she read storybooks to me and later to my sister. Not only was she giving her time to us, assuring us of her love, but she was also opening a wide world of discovery and opportunity to us. A mother, by simply reading to her children . . ."

Deborah's thoughts dwelled on the image of a mother reading to her little boy, a little boy who looked like Jason. It was no surprise to discover that the mother in her picture was her. An ache in her heart grew as she contemplated that child in her mind's eye. The child she wanted.

It had been an emotional day. Her concern and love for Manny and Elizabeth, the embrace Jason had given her, and now the image of his child, cuddled in her lap.

For two years she'd lived with almost no emotion. Now it flooded her life, rocking her foundations, making her hurt. As it had when Randall died.

But this time around, thanks to Jason, she'd learned not to hide. This time, when Jason left, she wouldn't withdraw from life. It was too short, too precious. This time, she'd keep a smile on her face, even though her heart would be breaking inside.

Applause broke through her thoughts. Jason returned to his seat beside her.

"Did I do okay?"

His teasing grin told her he just wanted her attention,

rather than needing reassurance. The audience's response told him *they* thought he'd done well.

"Yes, of course," she said, smiling, and picked up her water glass at once. She might love him. She might intend to be brave. But she wasn't masochistic. Keeping their contact to a minimum was her goal.

After the banquet ended, they greeted attendees for almost half an hour. Deborah tried to stay in the background, but Jason insisted she be introduced to everyone. A strong arm around her kept her by his side the entire time.

When finally they were able to escape to his car, Deborah sank back against the leather seat with a sigh.

"Was that exhaustion or pleasure?" Jason murmured, sliding the key into the ignition.

"I'm afraid it was exhaustion. I shouldn't have worn these shoes," she said, slipping her feet out of the heels that had plagued her while they stood.

"But they made your legs look even better than usual," he teased, his voice a caress that awakened every ounce of her being.

Her cheeks flushed, she turned to look out the window, offering some inane comment about the weather to distract him.

Jason allowed her to rattle on for several minutes, concentrating on his driving as he maneuvered his way through the crowded parking lot.

Once they were on their way, he said, "You know, I think I've made a mistake."

"Oh?" She didn't know what he was talking about.

"Well, maybe I mean a miscalculation rather than a mistake."

"About what?"

"Our arrangement."

She felt as if the wind had been knocked out of her. Trying to collect her thoughts, she turned to look at him. "You want to stop our—our agreement?"

"Hell, no! I'm perfectly happy with everything. I'm the envy of the entire town."

Deborah didn't even acknowledge his compliment. She simply waited for him to continue.

"It's you I'm worried about."

She'd given herself away! He knew she was in love with him. What now? Was he going to explain to her that he wasn't interested in anything permanent? She already knew that. She closed her eyes in pain.

"You're not benefitting from our arrangement."

"I don't understand." Maybe, just maybe, he hadn't figured out her secret. She held her breath.

He kept his eyes on the road, his voice even, as if he, too, were discussing the weather. "The whole idea, for you, at least, was to simulate dating, so you'd have the experience necessary to write the column."

"But I am. I mean, I've gone out more in the past few days than most women do in a month."

"You've gone out, yes, but you haven't *dated.*"

"What do you mean?"

He didn't answer at once as he pulled into her driveway. Then he turned to look at her. "If this were a real date, if I'd asked you out to, say, a movie or to dinner, how would it end?"

She caught her breath as she pictured such a scene. Shivers ran over her, and she almost jumped from her skin when he touched her, integrating reality and her dreamworld. "I'd say goodnight," she assured him in clipped tones, afraid he'd see her desire.

"And that proves my point. Come on." Without waiting for an answer, he got out of the car.

It took several seconds before Deborah could even move. His abrupt action had left her behind. As she reached for the car door, Jason was already there, pulling it open. She got out. Closing the door behind her, he swept her forward, his arm around her shoulders.

"What are you doing?"

"I'm going to rectify my mistake."

"What mistake?"

"I'll show you."

When they reached her front door, she turned around and looked up at him. "Thank you for—"

"Inside."

She blinked several times. "What?"

"I said, inside. If we were dating, you'd invite me inside."

"But we're not dating," Deborah protested, panic rising in her.

"I know. That's why we have to change things."

"No. No, I don't want to change things."

"But we have to, Deb. Let's go inside and I'll explain."

Deborah didn't want him to come into her house, but she didn't feel she had a choice. Either she'd go ballistic and he'd figure out what was wrong, or she'd agree to his calm suggestion.

Unlocking the door, she entered the house, immediately punching the code on the security system.

"This is the first time I've been in your home," Jason murmured, following her in. He strolled past her to look at the living room.

Deborah was justifiably proud of her home. Randall had been raised in a formal setting, afraid to relax in his mother's house. He'd delighted in the informal yet elegant surroundings Deborah had created.

"Nice, Deborah. You have a real talent for making a home."

"Thanks."

He moved over to look at a painting hanging over the couch. "This looks like an Impressionist painting. It's not, is it?"

"No, a copy. We bought it in Paris on our honeymoon. It's an imitation for the tourists, but I like it." They'd been so happy then.

"In Montmartre?" he asked, grinning at her again. "I love to visit that part of Paris. It's such a mix of tourist and bohemian."

Deborah relaxed a fraction. Perhaps he only intended to spend a little time in her home, having conversation.

"Aren't you going to offer me a cup of coffee?"

Jerked from her contemplation, Deborah hesitated. "I didn't think you'd want any. I mean, it's late and—"

"It's nine-thirty, Deb. I'm not that old."

"No, of course not, but there's no need for you to linger." It was too dangerous.

He walked to her side and slid his warm hand against her cheek, wrapping a finger around a strand of hair. "That's what we've got to talk about. Go make the coffee."

She fled to the kitchen, hoping to escape the desire his touch aroused.

Instant coffee would make the evening end earlier, she reasoned, quickly assembling a tray for serving. Her mind was in chaos as she considered what Jason had in mind.

She entered the den and set the tray on the coffee table before summoning Jason from the living room. "I thought we'd be more comfortable in here," she explained.

He surveyed the den, a satisfied look on his face. "Very nice. Even more to my taste." He approached one of the leather sofas, a deep wine in color. "You even have a big-screen TV. I don't suppose you like baseball?"

"I love baseball."

He sent her a crooked grin that tempted her heart. "My kind of woman." He'd used that expression when he'd taken her to lunch that first day. She'd rejected it then. She had to reject it now, to preserve her sanity.

With a shake of her head, she circled the coffee table and sat down on the matching sofa to the one he stood beside. "Your coffee," she offered, pouring a cup for him.

He abandoned the first sofa and joined her. After taking the cup from her, he set it on the coffee table.

"Is something wrong with the coffee?"

"Not a thing. But we have something more important to discuss." He leaned back and put an arm on the back of the sofa. "If I were a date, what would happen now?"

"Jason, we're not dating, and I see no need to pretend that we are." She leaned forward, hoping to avoid his touch.

"Deb, when I said we could meet each other's needs by going out together, I was right about me, but not about you."

"That's not true."

"As long as I escort you to these public functions and then bring you home, treating you like my sister, you're not getting any dating experience," he continued, ignoring her protest.

She pressed her lips firmly together. By dating experience he meant passion. Unfortunately, she felt passion every time she was near the blasted man. Jumping from the sofa, she stalked across the room, frantically searching for something to distract him.

He followed her.

"If I were a date, Deborah, you wouldn't get off with a handshake. In fact, you wouldn't get off with a kiss at the door." He drew closer, reaching out for her.

"No, Jason. This isn't a good idea," she said, as she backed up, pushing his hands away. "I don't need this kind of experience."

Her efforts didn't deter him. Before she know it, Deborah found herself back in the embrace she'd hungered for, dreamed of, wanted. Even though she told herself she couldn't want it, she did. "Jason—"

She said nothing else. His lips hungrily covered hers, his arms wrapping her against his warmth, and she was lost in the embrace of the man she loved.

Eleven

Big mistake.

Jason shuddered as Deborah, instead of resisting his embrace, leaned into him and wrapped her arms around his neck. Her lips molded to his, their softness inviting him, inciting him.

His hands stroked her back, one sliding to cup her hip, pressing her closer. The other tangled in her silken hair as his tongue sought entrance to her mouth, wanting more intimacy. There was no hesitancy on her part. She met him at every stage.

That's why he *knew* he'd made a big mistake.

He'd wanted Deborah almost from the beginning. Her reluctance had proven a deterrent to his desire. Now there was nothing to stop him from taking what he wanted . . . except his conscience.

Pulling his lips from hers, he buried her face into his chest, trying to remove temptation as he gasped for breath. "Deb . . . Deborah, we need to stop this."

She stiffened in his arms and then pulled from his embrace, immediately turning her back on him. He wanted to see her face, her eyes, and reached for her to turn her around.

"No!" she gasped, escaping him to cross the room.

Maybe it was for the best. He took in huge gulps of air, trying to control his response to her. She was the most incredible woman. With one look, she could destroy all his control.

Once he had his breathing back to normal, he said, "Deborah, I'm—"

"You'd better—"

They stopped. Their glances skittered away from each other. Jason took a step toward her and then halted.

"Let me apologize, Deb. I didn't mean to let things get out of hand. I don't think it's been a secret that—that you—that I want you. I thought I could control a simple embrace, but I was wrong." *Simple, hell. That kiss should've been registered on the Richter scale.*

"I don't think your—your theory is a good idea. I can manage to answer any letters that come in. If not, I'll ask for help."

"I'll give you any assistance you need."

"Not you!" she gasped, horrified. "I meant I'd ask someone who's dating. Or a psychologist, or someone."

"Fine. I'd better be going." If he didn't, he'd grab her again. Just standing in the same room with her was driving him crazy. He wanted her so badly he could hardly think.

She made no objection, following him to the door at a safe distance. He turned and looked at her. "I enjoyed the evening. You were wonderful, as usual."

"Thank you." She avoided his gaze.

He couldn't walk out the door. When he just stood there, saying nothing, she finally looked up. "Good night."

"Deb, why did you respond?"

Her cheeks flooded with color and she stared at her foot. His gaze followed hers and he almost groaned aloud. She'd left her shoes in the other room. Somehow, her stockinged toes looked as sexy as hell.

"It's been a long time."

Her whisper shook him from his contemplation of her toes. He couldn't resist reaching out to caress her cheek once more. "I hope I didn't upset you."

After a quick glance at him, she dropped her gaze again, but she didn't pull away from his touch. "No."

"You took me by surprise," he murmured, moving a step closer. "You need to, uh, work on your resistance if you're ever going to date again."

"I—I will."

"That kind of response is an open invitation. If I didn't have a conscience, we'd be in your bedroom right now." And he'd be a lot happier.

"I know."

"Maybe I should kiss you goodnight, since I'm leaving anyway, just for practice." She said nothing, keeping her head down.

He gave her at least thirty seconds to stop him. Well, maybe it was more like five, but he did wait. When she neither spoke nor moved, he pulled her back into his arms, feeling as if a lost part of him had come home.

His lips took hers and immediately their embrace deepened. There were no preliminaries this time. He buried himself in her sweetness, her warmth.

Deborah's surprise when he reached for the first button on her dress brought him back to reality. He didn't waste time on apologies or goodbyes. He exited her house as if it were on fire. Or he was on fire.

The woman sent him up in flames every time he touched her.

If she hadn't stopped him . . .

He would've stopped, of course. Wouldn't he?

Damn his conscience.

Deborah wasn't terribly surprised when Brenda, Jason's secretary, called her the next morning, just after Deborah arrived at work, to tell her Jason had to cancel their plans that evening.

He was embarrassed to face her.

Afraid she'd seduce him if they were alone.

Her teeth sank into her bottom lip, and she fought to hold back the tears. After a sleepless night, she'd promised herself she wouldn't run away and hide.

Instead, Jason was.

All this time she'd been trying to make him keep his distance. All she had had to do was kiss him. With all her heart.

She stared at her desk before doing an abrupt about face and leaving her office. She'd already turned in her column for the week. The only reason she'd come in had been to see what Jason would do. And so she couldn't call herself a coward.

Elizabeth wanted her to wear a pink dress for the wedding. She'd spend her day shopping.

"Did you get hold of Deborah?" Jason asked Brenda later that morning. He avoided his secretary's gaze, studying the papers in his hand intently.

"Yes, I did."

"Did she have any questions?"

"No. I just told her you had to cancel this evening. You're not going to the Mayor's dinner party?"

"No, something came up."

"Have you called the Mayor's office? I can do that for you, if you want."

"No, thanks, Brenda," Jason said, nodding vaguely in her direction. "I've taken care of it."

Yeah, he'd taken care of it. Just like he took care of everything last night. How dumb could he be? He'd thought he could demonstrate a few dating techniques of a guy on the make, educate Deborah. Instead, he'd plunged off a cliff, totally out of control, and he didn't know what to do now.

He had nothing to offer her.

He wasn't going to hang around, buy a house, start a

family. He was heading for the big time just as soon as he could. If he let his attraction to Deborah take over, he'd have her in bed before she knew what was going on. And then he'd leave her.

He hadn't made any secret of his plans. But Deborah might forget what he'd said in the heat of the moment. And that would be taking advantage.

Or getting caught.

Because *he* might forget his plans, too. And that scared him most of all.

Deborah didn't go into the office the next day, Friday. If Jason wanted to cancel the Friday night plans, a sports banquet at a local high school, he'd have to call her at home.

All day she puttered around the house, reorganizing a bookcase, filing recipes, watering her plants, listening for the phone to ring. When it didn't, she also worried about what to wear that evening. And how to behave with Jason.

At six-thirty, she was already dressed in a midnight-blue cocktail dress, her hair in wild curls, her make-up done to perfection, waiting for Jason to arrive.

She'd given herself numerous pep-talks about remaining cool and calm. No flirtatious looks, no suggestive remarks, and definitely no kisses.

The phone rang.

If Jason Bridges was daring to cancel now, after she'd waited all day, she'd boil him in oil. She stalked to the phone, seething when she recognized the voice on the line.

"Deb, it's Jason." When she said nothing, trying to contain her anger, he said, "Deb? Are you there?"

"I'm here."

"Listen, I got caught in a meeting. Could you meet me at the high school? I don't have time to get dressed and pick you up, too."

She relaxed slightly.

"Shall I call a taxi?"

"That'll take too long. Just drive your car and I'll follow you home to be sure you arrive safely."

"Fine."

"That's okay, isn't it? I'm really sorry, but—"

"I'll see you there." She hung up the phone even as he continued to apologize. So, he'd found a way to avoid being alone with her. He was clever, she'd have to give him that. But he was a coward.

She couldn't be quite as hard on him as she wanted to be, since she'd been a coward for two years after Randall's death. But his avoidance of her gave her a sense of superiority that pleased her. He was afraid of her.

This evening, she'd show him he had nothing to fear from her.

Snatching up her evening bag, she hurried to her garage. She wanted to arrive before her erstwhile escort.

Jason got there about fifteen minutes after the banquet should have started. He hoped Deborah had made his apologies for him.

Rushing into the school cafeteria, he found the crowd just taking their seats. A group of tables had been set on a dais at the front of the big room, and he spotted Deborah at once, stunningly beautiful in a dark blue dress that exposed her creamy shoulders.

Gulping, he moved in her direction. The evening was going to be a test of his concentration. And his self-control.

"Mr. Bridges, just in time," the principal boomed out as he saw him. "We were going to flip a coin to see who got your seat beside the lovely Deborah. It was either that or the guys were going to come to blows."

"I'm glad I arrived in time to avoid bloodshed." His words were cool, but his gaze burned into the faces of the men surrounding *his* date.

Deborah hadn't acknowledged his arrival yet. She was laughing at a whispered comment by a young man beside her who looked like he could compete for a Mr. America title. Jason considered the muscles bulging beneath the man's tuxedo to be a bit much, but it didn't appear Deborah agreed.

"Deborah, sorry I'm late." He draped his arm around her shoulders to be sure the other men got the message. Muscles frowned at him.

"Oh, hello, Jason. Have you met Bruce, John, Dennis and . . . oh, dear, is it Ed? Yes, that's right." The last man beamed at her as if she'd just saved the world.

"Good evening, gentlemen. Thank you for entertaining Deborah until I arrived." He pulled her toward the seats waiting for them at the head table.

"That wasn't very gracious of you, particularly after coming in late," she whispered even as she smiled over her shoulder at the men they left behind.

"I didn't feel gracious toward a bunch of high school students flirting with my date."

"That was the coaching staff, as you very well know." With a wicked smile, she added, "I'd already checked out the hunks in the student body."

So, that was the way she was going to behave, was it? As if he meant nothing to her? Well, he'd just—he stopped himself. Wasn't that what he wanted? Hadn't he told himself he needed to convince Deborah those kisses Wednesday night had meant nothing?

Yeah, but he hadn't expected such cooperation from her. He hadn't bought her excuse that she'd responded because it had been a long time since she'd been kissed.

She was attracted to him. Just like he was attracted to her. He looked at her, her shoulders bare, her breasts filling the sparkly bodice, her golden curls flirting every time she moved her head. Yeah, he was attracted to her. And she was attracted to him!

But she intended to convince him that he meant nothing to her. Ha! Just let her try.

By the end of the meal, he was ready to raise a white flag. Deborah had spent most of the dinner flirting with Muscles, who'd grabbed the chair on her right side.

Jason's attempts at dinner conversation had received short shrift.

"Did you work on the column today?"

"No." She turned back to her friend.

"Did you talk to Manny and Elizabeth today?"

"No."

"Did it rain today?"

She looked at him, wide-eyed. "No."

Okay, so he was desperate. He couldn't come up with a single topic to hold her attention. Especially when the guy next to her kept leaning toward her, touching her arm, her shoulder, staring at her.

Jason couldn't even hear their conversation because they were whispering. And the damned chicken tasted like sawdust! By the time he stood to give his speech, he was so angry he thought he had lockjaw from grinding his teeth.

When the banquet finally ended, he found himself caught in a crowd of well-wishers, while Deborah was once again surrounded by every eligible bachelor on the staff. When he saw Muscles pull out a pen to write something down, he brushed aside those around him with an apology and headed for Deborah.

"Time to go, Deb," he announced loudly.

"Is it? I've had such a lovely time. Thank you for being such gracious hosts."

Much to Jason's disgust, her audience practically melted at her feet in their rush to assure her of her welcome. As if it hadn't been obvious all evening.

"If you'd stop wearing such sexy dresses, you might not have guys slobbering all over you," he muttered grimly as they reached the parking lot. Damn, he hadn't meant to let her know about his jealousy.

Big blue eyes stared up at him briefly before she politely removed her arm from his hold. "I'm parked here. Thank you, Jason, for a lovely evening."

"I'm following you home, remember?"

"That's not necessary. I'm sure you're tired. I'll be just fine."

"I'm following you home," he ground out and yanked open her car door for her.

"Fine. Follow me home." Her words were colder than a blizzard in Alaska. When he closed her car door, she flipped the door lock and then glared up at him. He didn't move and she started the motor, throwing the car into gear. He almost got his toes run over.

He hurried to his own car and rushed to exit the parking lot. She wasn't going to wait for him to catch up with her.

All the way to her house, he reviewed the evening. Deborah drew men like flies to honey. The more he thought about her behavior that evening, the angrier he grew.

She thought she could kiss his socks off and then ignore him. Kiss him as if he meant something to her and then flirt with every muscle-bound man she came across.

When she pulled into her driveway, he followed. Her garage door went up, activated by her automatic opener, and then closed after she drove in. He was effectively shut out.

Even angrier, he parked his car and got out. Almost at a dead run, acting like a teenager, he leaped to her front porch and leaned on the doorbell.

He could hear the distant echo of the chimes ringing through the house. Where was she? It was a big house, but not that big. Finally, he heard footsteps.

"Stop that!"

"Open up!"

"Go away, Jason. I don't want to talk to you."

"You don't want to talk! I didn't do anything. You're the one who acted like Mae West!"

The door he'd been leaning on was pulled open and he almost fell at her feet. Catching his balance on the door jamb, he glared down at her.

She didn't seem any more pleased with him. "If you're unhappy with my behavior, feel free to find another patsy to follow you around in adoration."

"The only adoration you showed tonight was to Muscles."

"Don't be ridiculous."

"You gave him your number."

"I did no such thing! He was going to give me *his* number."

"Oh."

"If that's all you wanted to know, goodnight, Jason."

"No! No, there's something else."

"What?" She stared up at him, gorgeous as always, her blue eyes wide, her lips full, and so soft. He couldn't help himself.

"I forgot to kiss you goodnight," he murmured, all anger forgotten as he pulled her into his arms.

Twelve

Deborah didn't expect to see Jason Saturday.

She was glad.

After their embrace Friday night, she needed time to gain some perspective.

She hadn't stopped him this time. When he'd reached for the zipper of her dress, she hadn't pulled away. Instead, her lips had nibbled on the strong column of his neck, her fingers had slid through his hair, and she'd pressed closer to him.

No, she hadn't stopped him.

He had stopped himself.

His fingers had left the zipper unmoved, and his lips had returned to hers for another mind-numbing kiss. Then he'd left.

Over and over she told herself he was just being honorable. After all, he'd never hidden the fact that he wasn't staying around.

But there was a niggling little flame of hope that she hadn't been able to extinguish. He'd been jealous of the football coach at the banquet. And he kissed her like a man out of control.

His kisses weren't practiced, suave seducers, trying to overcome any reluctance on her part. First of all, she'd offered no resistance.

No, they were all-consuming, total involvement, leaving

both of them panting, shaking, all to pieces. At least she *thought* Jason's reaction was like hers. He hadn't hung around too long for her to be sure.

And that was the most telling point. In spite of the flagrant encouragement she'd given him, Jason had run away as fast as he could.

She frightened him. And the only reason had to be his fear of falling in love with her. Just as she had fallen in love with him.

So, in spite of her repeated warnings to herself, hope flickered in her heart. Hope that perhaps Jason would find he didn't have the strength to leave her.

She had several more months to work on him.

Preparing for the wedding Sunday, Deborah perfected her appearance with Jason in mind, not the newlyweds. In fact, she scarcely even considered the couple who'd dominated her thoughts before Jason arrived on the scene.

Other than to hope that she, too, would find happiness. Like Manny and Elizabeth.

Her gown, a dusty rose with a sweetheart neckline, sheer sleeves and a flowing skirt, was matched by the broad-brimmed hat, giving her a southern belle look. She added matching silk pumps and looked at herself in the mirror.

The doorbell interrupted her study. She licked her lips, knowing it was Jason. Her fingers were shaking in her excitement, her hope.

Hurrying to the door, she swung it open and smiled at him. He was dressed in a tux and looked incredibly handsome. "Hi, Jason."

Even though she stopped back for him to enter, he remained on the porch. "Are you ready to go? I'm a little late."

She checked her watch but didn't argue with him even when she discovered he was early. "Yes. Just let me get my bag, and I'll be ready."

He nodded but didn't answer. Her excitement was slowly

dying. Perhaps she'd been wrong. If he wouldn't even talk to her, maybe he wasn't falling in love with her.

They were both in a solemn mood as they drove to Elizabeth's house. What little conversation they had centered on Manny and Elizabeth.

"Where are they going to live after the honeymoon?" Jason asked after a long silence.

"In Elizabeth's house. Manny lives in an apartment."

"He doesn't mind?"

"I don't think so. He knows Elizabeth would hate to give up her gardening." She slanted a look at him and then turned her attention to the scene out her window. "After all, he loves her. He wants to make her happy."

"Sometimes it's hard to know what to do."

Deborah turned to study Jason. He was staring at the road ahead of him, but she knew he was aware of her look. And she wasn't sure he was talking about Elizabeth and Manny.

"I think a person should do what his heart tells him to do," she said softly.

"I think a person's head is more reliable."

She drew a deep breath. "Well, Manny's head tells him Elizabeth has a nicer place to live than his apartment. Her home is larger and well-furnished. They couldn't possibly move all her belongings into Manny's apartment."

"So *he* should just fit into *her* life? Why shouldn't she make the adjustment?"

"She'll be making a lot of adjustments. They both will. But she offered to move into Manny's apartment. *He* chose for them to live in her house."

A growl was Jason's only response.

"That's what marriage is all about. Two people making adjustments so their lives can blend together."

"Oh, so now you're an authority on marriage?"

"More than you," she replied with exasperation. "At least *I've* been married."

All conversation ended.

When they reached Elizabeth's house, Deborah joined the bride in her bedroom and Jason rounded the house to enter the backyard, Elizabeth's rose garden.

"Oh, Deborah, I'm so excited," Elizabeth said, holding on to Deborah's hands. "The sun is shining and the roses are perfect!"

"And you look beautiful, Elizabeth. Is there anything I can do?"

"Just talk to me and keep me from getting nervous. Isn't it silly? I love Manny with all my heart, but I'm scared to death. Life is so strange!"

Deborah could only agree.

Jason stood to one side, watching the group of people milling about the chairs set up in front of a white canopy. He didn't know anyone here, except Manny, who was surrounded by a crowd, and Jason didn't feel like social chitchat.

It was a relief to be away from Deborah. When she'd answered the door, glowing in rosy pink, a big smile on her lips, he didn't think he could contain the desire that surged through him.

It wasn't just her beauty. Her smile lit something inside him, a faith that all was right with the world. When he was with her, he felt strong enough to leap tall buildings. Or make love to her forever.

But Deborah belonged in this kind of scene. A family wedding, friends, neighbors gathered to celebrate her happiness. He was returning to his first love, reporting. He was seeking adventure, truth, faraway places.

It scared him that those things didn't look as attractive as they once did. It was Deborah's fault. She built so much desire in him that he felt like a pressure cooker about to explode.

"Jason?"

He jerked around to discover Clare, the feature writer, and Pete, the photographer from the paper. "Hi. Glad you made it. Everything going all right?"

"Oh, yeah. We've already gotten a lot of photographs. And I had breakfast with the bride. Pete did double duty and had breakfast with the groom. We've got everything covered."

"Great. Uh, Deborah is with Elizabeth now."

"We know," Pete replied, grinning. "We got a couple of pictures of them together. Deborah sure looks good."

Jason nodded in agreement, drawing in a deep breath, instead of punching Pete out like he wanted to. He'd been wanting to hit *someone* since he'd left Muscles on Friday night.

"When is it going to start?" he asked, hoping to shift his attention away from Deborah.

Clare took his arm. "Right now. We'd better grab a seat." She waved the photographer away. "Go take pictures, Pete."

Jason sat in agony, watching Deborah come down the aisle, a bouquet of roses in her hands, a trembling smile on her lips. He wondered if she'd looked as beautiful at her own wedding.

"She looks great, doesn't she?" Clare whispered, watching his reaction.

"Yes," he returned and focused his gaze on Manny, who was nervously watching the back of the garden, beyond Deborah.

He didn't blame the guy for being nervous. If he were in his shoes, waiting for Deborah to come down—whoa! That wasn't going to happen.

The minister motioned for the guests to stand and the wedding march began in earnest. A radiant Elizabeth began the march down the aisle, her gaze on her future husband. Jason turned back to look at Manny again. He wasn't surprised to discover a blissful look on his face.

He understood.

After the ceremony, a crew of workers turned the garden into a delightful sidewalk cafe, setting up tables with pink umbrellas all over it. A long table was draped with a pink cloth and loaded down with food. At the very end stood an elegant wedding cake, four majestic white tiers with climbing roses delicately created from pink and green icing.

He reluctantly joined Deborah. His emotions were too near the surface for him to feel comfortable near her, but he had no choice. Quickly handing her a plate, he guided her to the serving line, hoping to concentrate on food.

"Where are we eating this evening?" she asked. "I don't want to spoil my appetite if we're going to Joe T. Garcia's." Deborah smiled up at him and then turned toward the food.

Jason stood stock still. She looked over her shoulder and then took a step back to him.

"Jason? You didn't answer."

"It's a secret. Just don't eat too much," he assured her with a smile, probably the first one he'd given her all day.

He was in big trouble. He'd forgotten the lie he'd told Deborah on Monday when he'd been trying to discover what her plans were for Sunday. There was no old friend in Fort Worth who'd invited them out to dinner.

Now what was he going to do? Admit to Deborah he'd lied? He didn't want to do that, even though he should be glad to avoid her. No, he'd think of something.

When the call came for all single women to gather for the tossing of the bouquet, Deborah didn't move. But Clare, having joined her and Jason for the buffet, grabbed her arm.

"Come on, Deborah. I'm not missing this opportunity."

Since Jason was nowhere around, Deborah shrugged her shoulders and followed Clare. He'd excused himself several minutes earlier and approached Elizabeth before entering the house.

It seemed most of the female guests were single. Pete started taking pictures and Deborah drifted to the back of the pack. She'd been in enough pictures today.

"Where's Deborah?" Elizabeth called out.

Several ladies pushed Deborah forward.

"Oh, there you are. Okay, I'm ready."

Elizabeth turned her back and tossed her bouquet. Deborah realized Elizabeth wanted her to catch it. The bride had made several remarks about Deborah and Jason. Deborah was unable to decide what to do. But when the bouquet came straight toward her, something inside had her reaching out for the promise the roses would bring.

Crash!

The seventy-year-old beside her had no intention of letting her catch the bouquet. Almost knocking Deborah to the ground, the white-haired lady grabbed the roses and let out a loud whoop.

Deborah staggered several feet before regaining her balance. The lady who caught the bouquet smiled at her. "I hope you're all right, honey. Sorry to be so rough, but you've got a lot more time left than I do."

Strong arms encircled her.

"Are you okay?" Jason asked.

She sank back against him, willing to face a crowd of rabid women if it meant he touched her again. He'd studiously avoided any contact all day.

"I'm fine."

"Now, all single men!" Manny called out.

Jason hesitated but Clare, standing beside them, shoved him toward the others. "Go on, Jason. It'll be fun."

There weren't nearly as many single men at the wedding as there were women. And Manny's aim was better than Elizabeth's. Jason didn't have to move a step to catch the garter Manny had removed from Elizabeth's leg. It just fell into Jason's hands.

Deborah shivered when Jason turned to glare at her. It

wasn't her fault. But she couldn't shout her innocence across the rose garden. So, with a cool smile, she turned her back on him and began talking to the octogenarian next to her.

After several minutes of shouted conversation, she was relieved to be interrupted by Clare.

"Elizabeth wants you to help her change."

Deborah excused herself from her new friend and hurried to the house. It wasn't until she was closing the door behind her that she looked for Jason. He was still glaring at her.

With a sigh, she let the door close and tried to concentrate on Elizabeth. Half an hour later, she stood with the rest of the guests, waving goodbye to the happy couple. Somehow, the joyous occasion was ending on a depressing note.

Jason clearly felt she was trying to trap him into marriage. He hadn't come near her since he caught the garter.

What was she to do now?

She mentally composed a letter to Dear Deborah. If she received a letter like that, what would she say? Stay calm. Act as if you don't care, even though your heart is breaking. You don't want him if he doesn't want you. By his own choice.

Good advice. Too bad it hurt so much.

"Ready?"

A grim Jason stood beside her, looking everywhere but at her.

"Yes, of course, but I could probably catch a ride with Clare if you have a busy schedule today." Ah, she was proud of her nonchalant air.

"Don't be ridiculous!" he snapped back. Without another word, he took her arm and marched her to his car.

"Really, Jason, there's no need to act as if I'd spit in your face."

He assisted her into his car and didn't respond to her comment until he was behind the steering wheel. "I don't know what you're talking about."

"Yes, you do." She swallowed her tears. "You've been

angry ever since Manny tossed you the garter. Just for the record, I had nothing to do with it."

"I never said you did." He wheeled out of the driveway with a screech of his tires.

"I don't need that kind of help to make someone want to marry me," she continued, trying to keep her voice from trembling.

"I know that!" he yelled, his hands almost white from clenching the steering wheel.

The tense silence that followed wasn't like the other times they'd driven without talking. There was no sense of camaraderie, no relaxation, no anticipation. Deborah fought back tears. It hurt to accept his rejection of her. Because he had rejected her as clearly as if he'd shouted it from the rooftop.

"There's no need to walk me to the door," Deborah said tightly, opening her door. "I can manage."

"I insist," he ground out, swinging his own door open.

They came face to face in front of the car, but Deborah just stepped around him and hurried up her front walk.

"Deborah," he called just before she slipped inside and slammed the door in his face.

"What?"

"I'll pick you up at five-thirty."

"I really don't think that's a good idea. Why don't you just tell your friend that I—I had a headache!"

"I'll pick you up at five-thirty," he repeated in a determined voice, "and you'd better be ready." Without waiting for her agreement, he turned and stalked down the walk to his car.

Deborah leaned her face against the door and watched him drive away, tears sliding down her cheeks. This time, he was coming back. But she knew in her heart that the time was coming when he wouldn't.

Thirteen

Casual. Jason said dress casually, and Deborah did. But she wasn't going to make things easy on the man. If she was going to suffer, then he should too.

She wore a soft blue vee neck sweater and jeans. Tight jeans. And she used her most expensive perfume. Her hair was loose and curly, her makeup soft. If he was determined to reject her, let him know what he'd be missing.

Tonight, she wasn't going to cry. She was going to smile and flirt and have fun. She was going to pretend there was no tomorrow. *Then* she was going to come home and cry. After Jason left her.

She groaned even as she practiced her smile in the mirror. Hopefully the couple they were dining with would be fun. She didn't even know their names.

When the doorbell rang, she drew a deep breath, reminding herself of her promises, and then grabbed her shoulder bag and headed to the front door. No invitation to come in for Jason Bridges. He wanted her ready and she was ready.

"Hi, Jason," she said breezily as she opened the door and then closed it behind her. "I'm ready."

There was a frown on his face as he studied her, and she wondered if she'd forgotten anything important. Determined to carry on, she raised her chin and smiled brilliantly. "Ready?"

"Yeah."

She hurried ahead of him and was already around the car and in the passenger seat by the time Jason reached the driveway.

After he got in the car, she said, "You haven't told me the names of the people we're dining with. Was it the husband you went to school with?"

"Yeah, well, uh, I have something to tell you," Jason said as he backed out of the driveway and started the car forward.

"Yes?"

"There is no old friend."

Shaken from her cheerfulness, Deborah stared at him. "What?"

"I made them up. I'm sorry. I wanted to know what you were doing Sunday, since you were being so secretive, and, well, I made them up."

"Then why didn't you tell me the truth today?"

"I figured I owed you a meal for lying."

The vivacity she'd conjured up disappeared. "Take me home, Jason."

"Come on, Deb. I've made plans."

"I want to go home. You owe me nothing." She'd promised herself she wouldn't cry. She clenched her fingers tightly trying to keep that promise.

"I can't do that. When you asked me about where we were going, I called Rachel. She's cooking for the four of us."

"Call and tell her I got sick."

"Deb, she's all excited about us coming over." When Deborah didn't respond, he added, "Paul says your friendship has helped Rachel over a hard time . . . again. I never did thank you for being with her when she lost the baby."

He was making it almost impossible to keep her promise not to cry. "Rachel's my friend."

"I know. And she's waiting for us now." No response again. "Shall I take you home?"

She closed her eyes and gnawed on her bottom lip. Finally, she whispered, "No."

They drove almost an entire block before he said, "Thank you, Deborah."

The rest of the trip was in silence.

Jason put down his napkin with a sigh. His sister had always been a good cook. "That was terrific, Rachel."

"Thank you, big brother. More cake?"

"Absolutely not. I'm going to have to run an extra mile as it is."

"Deb?"

"No, thanks, Rachel. But it was delicious. The entire dinner was marvelous. I need to take cooking lessons from you."

"Oh, you can't con me," Rachel teased. "Don't believe a word of it, Jason. She's a great cook." With a sideways look at her brother, Rachel added, "Deborah has a lot of talents."

Paul leaned forward. "Rachel, don't you think it's time for some coffee?"

Jason breathed a sigh of relief as Rachel agreed with her husband and got up from the table. Deborah immediately joined her.

"You guys go in the den and we'll bring the coffee in there. We're going to play Trivial Pursuit." Rachel didn't wait for complaints.

Once the ladies had left them, Jason looked at Paul. "Thanks for trying to distract her."

"You're welcome, but we both know she's like a terrier when she's intent on something."

"I know. You never had a chance of getting away," Jason replied.

Paul grinned, but his tone was serious when he said,

"Thank God. She's the best thing that ever happened to me."

Jason slapped him on the shoulder as they moved into the den. "I'm glad you feel that way."

"You should try it." Paul noted the glare on Jason's face. "Oops. I promise, Jason, I didn't intend—well, hell, I was just being honest."

"I know, pal, but my sister is a bulldozer on her own. She doesn't need any help."

Throughout the dinner, Rachel had been pitching Deborah as wife material. If he'd thought for a minute Deborah had planned it that way, he'd be furious. But she was more embarrassed than him.

When she'd met him at the door, bubbling sunshine all over the place, he'd wondered if she'd had too much champagne at the reception. But ever since he admitted his lie, she'd been quiet. Too quiet.

It made him want to cuddle her in his arms and promise she'd never be hurt again. He wanted to kiss her fears away. He wanted to do things that he didn't have any right to do. Because he wasn't willing to accept the consequences.

He sighed.

"Looking forward to Trivial Pursuit?"

"Do we have to play that game?" Jason asked.

"You'd better not complain. She has some others that ask a lot of personal questions. Especially about the woman you're with and how you feel about her. You're better off with Trivial Pursuit."

Jason stared at Paul. "You're kidding."

"Nope. Ah, here comes the coffee."

The two ladies carried in a tray and a game box.

"Here's Trivial Pursuit," Rachel sang out. "Or, if you don't like that game, I have some new ones we could try." She looked right at Jason.

"I'm dying to play Trivial Pursuit," he assured her, with Paul's words in mind. "I haven't played it in ages."

"Are you sure? I thought you didn't like it, Jason."

"Not me. I love it. Shall we play guys against the girls?" He smiled, trying to look enthusiastic.

"No, with just four of us, I don't think we need teams." Rachel kept watching him, suspicion in her eyes.

They started playing, each trying to answer the questions. Gradually, Deborah seemed to relax, a smile occasionally lighting her lips.

Jason watched her covertly, regretting the change in her since he picked her up. He didn't want to make her unhappy. When she smiled, the world seemed a wonderful place.

"Jason, your turn," Rachel reminded him.

"Oh, right." He rolled the dice and moved his game piece. "Entertainment."

Deborah pulled the card and looked at the question he had to answer. "Oh, this is too easy!"

"Let me see," Rachel insisted, leaning over her shoulder. "You're right. Let's find a harder one."

"Hey, none of that. You're not playing fair."

"Thanks, Paul, for standing up for me," Jason said.

"You guys always hang together," Rachel complained. "Okay, Deb, read him the question."

"Who was the Lone Ranger's sidekick?"

Jason grinned and then pretended to worry over the answer. "Um, gee, I'm not sure. Uh, could it be . . . Tonto?"

"Show off," Deborah replied. They grinned at each other for the first time the entire evening.

"Isn't this fun? I just love all of us being together," Rachel sang out, a big grin on her face.

The smile disappeared from Deborah. She picked up the dice and handed them to Jason. "Your turn again."

It was almost eleven before Jason felt he could call an end to the evening. In spite of everything, he'd had a good time. Rachel was right. It was fun, all of them together.

"Thanks again for dinner, Rachel. It was wonderful."

"Anytime, Deb. I'll talk to you tomorrow."

The two men shook hands and then Jason led Deborah to his car. And silence. She made no attempt at conversation on the way home. And he couldn't think of a thing to say.

When he stopped the car in her driveway and reached for the door, she spoke. "No. Don't get out. Thank you for the evening, but I don't intend to go out with you anymore. I think you need to find someone else to escort to any public functions. Or anywhere else. Goodnight, Jason."

"Wait, Deb. What about your writing?" Why was he asking that? She was right. They shouldn't be together anymore. Why couldn't he just turn loose of her?

"If you don't like my writing, you have the right to fire me." Without another word, she got out of the car and walked away. He waited until she entered the house and clicked on a light. Then he drove away.

All the way to his apartment, he relived the time spent with Deborah. He wanted her. More than that, he was afraid he was falling in love with her. He could hardly be around her with putting his hands on her. She dominated his thoughts no matter where he was. He wanted to take care of her.

The nesting instinct was growing stronger and stronger. But he didn't want to settle down. He was a big-time reporter, traveling the world. He was accomplishing what his father had only dreamed about. Marriage and children had stopped the elder Bridges.

If Jason married Deborah, he'd end up like his father. Staid, settled, comfortable. Not out there on the edge. He'd probably get a spare tire around his middle like his father. And fall asleep watching the ten o'clock news. Was that what he wanted?

Of course not.

He wanted Deborah.

But he didn't want the ties that came with her.

By the time he reached his apartment, he'd made a decision. It was too late to make the phone calls he needed to make tonight. But first thing in the morning, he was going to make some changes.

Deborah wasn't eager to go into the office the next morning. In fact, she wasn't eager to do anything. The temptation was there to just curl into a ball under the covers and hide.

Her brave face the night before had quickly disappeared. When Jason had finally driven her home, she knew she couldn't pretend anymore. So there would be no more outings with Jason. She had to begin this morning rebuilding her life without him.

At least he had taught her not to hide, to try to run away from the pain. She wouldn't repeat her mistakes of two years ago. That's why she was wearing a red suit this morning, to appear cheerful. And she carefully kept a smile pasted on her face as she greeted other workers this morning.

It was ten o'clock by the time she settled behind her desk, ready to check out the letters received that morning for her column. She had just started reading the first one when Madge, the reporter in the cubicle next to her stuck her head in Deborah's door.

"Hey, do you know anything?"

"Oh, hi, Madge. No, nothing. What's going on?"

"Rats. We hoped you'd know. After all, you've been going out with him a lot."

"What are you talking about?" A sinking sensation was filling her.

"The boss. He didn't come in this morning."

Worry wiped away her resistance to thoughts of Jason. "Has anyone checked to see if he's all right?"

"Yeah, Brenda talked to him. But he said he had some things to do and wouldn't be in until later. It's just not like him, though. He's always here early."

"Madge, you should be writing fiction," Deborah muttered, breathing a sigh of relief. "I'm sure nothing's wrong. Everybody has an off day. That's all it is."

"Okay. I'll pass the word along. I'm sure you know better than the rest of us."

Madge disappeared before Deborah could protest her assumption. Well, everyone would notice soon. She wouldn't have to tell them about the change in Jason's social life. Word would spread quickly.

She considered calling his office, just to make sure everything was all right. But she talked herself out of it. It was just like she told Madge. He was having an off day.

And even if something was wrong, it had nothing to do with her. She'd made that clear last night. Of course, it wouldn't hurt to call Rachel, just to tell her again how lovely the dinner was last night.

Before she could get cold feet, Deborah picked up the phone and called her friend. When the answering machine clicked on, she put down the receiver. Everything was fine. She had to believe that.

After half an hour of trying to work, she dialed Rachel's number again. Still no answer. She was debating calling Brenda, knowing she wouldn't be able to work until she knew Jason was all right, when she looked up to find him leaning against her door jamb.

A sense of *déjà vu* struck her as he stood there, ridiculously handsome in his casual clothes, his dark hair brushed back from his forehead, his hands in his pockets.

"Hello, Jason."

"Deborah."

Neither smiled. Deborah waited for him to speak. Finally, he moved over to the chair in front of her desk.

"Is everything all right?"

"Everything's fine. I just need to talk to you."

When he sat there, saying nothing, staring at her desk as if seeking something, she asked, "What?"

He looked up then, and Deborah suddenly knew. He was

leaving. Why or how she didn't know. But she knew he was leaving.

"I'm not going to stay six months like I said. I'm—I'm leaving this afternoon. I thought I should tell you."

In a low voice, trying to control the emotions that surged through her, she asked, "Where are you going?"

"I'm going to New York, first. Then I'll go on special assignment for the *Times*. An old friend is the editor there, and he's offered me something at once."

Millions of questions raced through her mind, along with a desperate urge to beg him not to go. Deborah ignored all of it and tried to smile. She wasn't sure how successful she was. "Good luck."

"Thank you." He rubbed his bottom lip with his index finger, still staring at her desk. "Deborah, I never meant to hurt you," he finally said in a rush.

Deborah straightened her spine and raised her chin. Just a few more minutes of pretending to be strong, and he'd be gone. Then she could fall apart. Not now.

"Jason, we're both adults. I understand that you have to do what you think is best. I hope you'll be happy."

"Of course I will be. Reporting is my life. It's what I do best." His gaze flashed to her face and then away. He pushed himself up from the chair. "Thank you for being so understanding."

She didn't say anything. In fact, she didn't intend to say anything to him ever again. But as he turned to go, she couldn't hold back one more thing. "Jason? Take—take care of yourself."

His gaze fixed on her face for one long moment before he reached over the desk to graze her cheek with his fingers. "You, too," he whispered, and then he was gone.

Fourteen

"Deb?"

The voice on the phone was shaky, hesitant, so unlike Rachel that Deborah didn't recognize it at once.

"Rachel? Is that you? What's the matter?"

"Oh, no! Don't tell me you haven't heard?" Rachel wailed. "I'm so sorry, Deb. I thought he'd stay. I had no idea he'd run away like this. I can't—"

Deborah interrupted the almost sobbing Rachel. "Rachel, don't be silly. You're not responsible for Jason's decision, and even if you were, it's not a tragedy."

Silence greeted her determined speech. Finally, Rachel said, "I'm proud of you, Deb. You're being strong. You won't go away again, will you?"

"No, I won't disappear. Jason taught me not to do that. So, you're stuck with me, kid. How about lunch one day this week?"

"I'd love to, but I'd rather you come to dinner tomorrow night. Mom and Dad are flying in today. Dad's going to check things out at the paper and interview the man Jason recommended for editor before he left yesterday. Would it be too much to ask you to join us?"

Deborah drew a deep breath, frantically searching for an excuse. But nothing came to mind. And she'd promised herself to be strong. "I'd love to come to dinner."

"Great. About seven."

Deborah hung up the receiver, her eyes closing. The pain was supposed to be easier to take if you faced it. She was sure she'd read that somewhere. Of course, he'd only been gone a few hours. How long would she have to wait to stop thinking about him, longing for him, worrying over him?

Days? Months? A sound escaped her lips that was a cross between a whimper and a laugh. More like years. All the years of her life. But surely it would dull, soften, become tolerable.

Because right now it hurt.

The next evening, Deborah dressed with care. She'd met the elder Bridges several times, but she hadn't seen them since Rachel's wedding.

Hopefully, the conversation would dwell on Rachel and Paul, rather than Jason, or she might have to leave early with an imagined, or possibly real, splitting headache.

Rachel answered the door, a glow on her face, and hurriedly escorted Deborah into the den.

"What's going on, Rachel?"

"I have some news, but I wanted to wait until you arrived." She turned loose of Deborah's arm and ran to Paul's side. "Now?"

"Now, sweetheart," he responded to his wife, his smile warm and loving.

"Mom, Dad, Deborah, we're expecting!" Rachel was practically hopping up and down, and Paul beamed.

Pandemonium reigned as everyone asked questions. Rachel assured them the doctor said her health was fine. Immediately, Mrs. Bridges took over the dinner, with Deborah assisting, and Paul and Mr. Bridges hovered over Rachel.

Deborah was truly happy for her friends. She was also pleased to have the focus of the evening so squarely off Jason. However, at the dinner table, that changed.

"Did you tell Jason before he left?" Mrs. Bridges asked when there was a pause in the conversation.

"No, I didn't." Momentarily, the joy was wiped from Rachel's face. "And I'm glad. He doesn't deserve to know."

Her parents, as well as Paul, seemed shocked by her words. It was Deborah, however, who remonstrated with her.

"Rachel, that's not fair. Jason did what he had to do. And he's always loved and supported you. He'll be just as happy for you as we are."

Tears filled Rachel's eyes. Immediately Paul left his chair to put his arm around her. "I know," she sniffed. "But I had hoped—" She buried her face in Paul's chest.

Mr. Bridges cleared his throat. "Here, now, Rachel. That has to be Jason's decision." An older version of his son, he turned to look at Deborah. "We just want you to know, Deborah, that we think he's an idiot to leave."

"I—he—I have nothing to do with—"

"Leon didn't mean to embarrass you, dear," Mrs. Bridges intervened. "We just want you to know that we count you as one of the family, and we wish the connection were closer." She rose from the table. "Now, it's time for dessert. If you two gentlemen will escort Rachel to the den, Deborah and I will serve the delicious carrot cake Rachel made this afternoon."

The sound of a machine gun pierced the air over Jason's head, but he ignored it. That intrusive noise had become commonplace since he'd arrived in Beirut. Perspiration ran down his chest, dampening the front of his shirt. The back of it, pressed against the wall of a crumbling building, was already soaked.

"What d'ya think?" a burly man beside him asked.

Jason wearily raised his gaze. "I think we're crazy to

have even tried this. An interview with those guys? They'd as soon shoot us as not."

"I guess you're right. But it seemed like a good idea at two o'clock this morning."

"I think that was the bourbon talking, Jim. You drank half a bottle last night."

"Hey, are you my old lady now?" the big man demanded. "You know, Bridges, since you came back, you're not the same. Where's that adventurin' spirit you used to have? I could always count on you to try something crazy."

"Maybe I'm too old," Jason said with a sigh.

"Nah. I'm thinkin' you're in love. You didn't even look at that skirt who waltzed in this morning from the Frankfort office. Last year you would've had a date for dinner before she even unpacked."

Jason glared at his friend, then ran a hand down his stubbly cheek, wiping away sweat and dirt. "I'm too tired to think about women." He shoved himself up. "Come on, let's get out of here."

The two men crawled along the wall, then darted across an alley and through to the next street where they'd left their vehicle. By the time they reached their small, dingy office, Jason convinced himself that it was just the dreariness of the surroundings, the exhaustion, the heat, the despair that had him regretting his decision to leave Fort Worth.

Certainly Jim was not right. He wasn't in love. That wasn't in his plans. Something would break in a few days and he'd feel that thrill of scooping a story. Adrenaline would flow and he wouldn't notice the miserable conditions.

As they entered the small room, the only other occupant was busy reading a letter. He looked up, waved a handful of envelopes and said, "Mail finally made it through without getting shot up."

Jason and his friend practically vaulted the desks and seized the mail, quickly dividing it between them. Settling behind his desk, Jason tore into the letters from his parents and his sister, his blood pumping, his surroundings forgotten.

He'd been here almost six weeks. Rachel had written him about her pregnancy, and his parents had passed on news about the paper. His father hadn't decided on a replacement yet, because the one man Jason had felt could handle it had accepted a job with the *New York Times*. He didn't blame him. That was too good an opportunity to pass up.

He loved reading the news from home. But, today, he finally admitted to himself what he searched for was news of Deborah. At first there had been almost nothing. Gradually, mention of her crept into Rachel's letters.

His mother wrote about Deborah most frequently. She was helping his parents find a house to buy and introducing his mother to a lot of people in Fort Worth.

His chest swelled with pride. Deborah hadn't quit. She was doing what needed to be done. He appreciated her efforts on behalf of his family. He always had. His leaving had nothing to do with his approval of her.

Her name caught his attention in his mother's letter. Ah, she'd joined them for dinner—he stopped, irritation filling him. Her date? Who was she dating? He reread his mother's words, but she didn't identify the male who'd accompanied Deborah.

He hoped the woman knew what she was doing. She was too potent to expect men to keep their hands off her. He grunted aloud as he remembered the times he had touched her. The thought of some other man caressing that soft skin, smiling into her blue eyes, made his stomach turn.

"Man, it's so hot," Jim growled. "Wanna go for a drink?"

"What?" Jason asked, frowning at the interruption.

Jim repeated his invitation.

"Maybe later. I've got some things to do."

He continued to sit at his desk long after the two other men had headed to the hotel where they were staying. His mother's letter remained gripped in his hand as he thought about Deborah, and the days he'd spent with her.

A smile played about his lips as he recalled her appearance at the reception for the previous editor. She'd certainly surprised him. But then, she did that every time they were together.

The phone rang, awakening him from his thoughts. After dealing with the caller, he stared at his surroundings. He'd left Deborah and come here to find excitement? He wanted to spend his days fighting danger, dirt and depression? He wanted to be alone?

Deborah sighed as she typed in the last word of her response. The woman writing to *Dear Deborah* had broken up with her boyfriend. She wanted to know what to do to make the pain go away. Deborah wore a grim smile as she reread her answer.

She should know. She'd tried all those things. Stay busy. Make new friends. Indulge yourself. Start an improvement plan, maybe a new exercise program. Get away from everyone and everything that reminded you of him.

The last item she'd listed she just couldn't bear to do. She couldn't cut herself off from Rachel and Paul, or Mr. and Mrs. Bridges, for that matter. And as long as she was around them, she couldn't forget Jason.

"Oh, get real, Townsend," she muttered derisively to herself. "You're not going to forget him no matter what you do."

Maybe not, she admitted with a sigh. But she wasn't going to quit trying. Because she worried too much about whether he was safe, happy, in love with another woman. And she was getting dark circles under her eyes from not sleeping well.

"Mrs. Townsend?"

She looked up to discover a young man who worked in the mailroom. "Yes, Billy?"

"I have a special delivery for you. It just came in."

He brought a bouquet of a dozen red roses in a tall vase from behind his back. A long white envelope was pinned to the ribbon.

Deborah frowned. She certainly hoped the flowers weren't from Peter, the man she'd been dating lately. He'd said he understood that she wanted to keep things light.

"Thanks, Billy. Just put them here on my desk."

The boy set the roses down and left. Deborah concentrated on the envelope. Unpinning it, she lifted the unsealed flap and withdrew a single sheet of paper.

Dear Deborah,

I need advice. I ran away from someone I love. Now I realize how much she means to me. Should I return and ask her to forgive me? Can I convince her that I only want to make her happy? Please tell me what to do.

Yours,
A Roving Reporter

Deborah read the signature again, then searched for a return address. As she did so, a movement at the door drew her gaze. Her breath caught in her throat and she wondered if she were dreaming. How many times had she imagined him there, like that, casually propped against her door jamb?

"Jason?" she whispered, doubt in her voice.

"Hi, Deb."

She closed her eyes and prayed that he was real, that she hadn't lost her mind. Her eyes popped open as he spoke again.

"Do you have any advice for me?"

She stared at him and then at the letter. Her gaze returned

to his strong, handsome face, and she swallowed the tears that were building in her throat.

"What are you doing here?"

"I told you, in the letter."

"You—you came back?"

"I'm no ghost, sweetheart."

"But why?"

He straightened from his stance and crossed the few feet to her desk. "That's a stupid question. I said in my letter why I came back. Is it too late?"

She closed her eyes again. Fear made it hard to believe that her dream might be real. Strong hands pulled her from her chair and around the desk before his lips covered hers. Her mind might not be able to take in his return, but her body responded at once. How she'd missed his touch.

With a groan, he broke off their kiss and buried his face in her neck. Tears were streaming down her cheeks as she wrapped her arms around him, determined to never let go. "You came back for me?"

He raised his head and looked down at her. "I'm never going to leave you again." The vow his words made was echoed in his eyes and Deborah caressed his cheek, rejoicing in touching what she had only dreamed about for the past six weeks.

"I'll pack. I can leave at once. Rachel and Paul can sell the house and—"

"Whoa! Sell the house? I like that house."

"But Jason, if I'm going to the Middle East with you—"

"You're doing no such thing!"

"I refuse to be a long distance wife! I'll—" she broke off as she realized he hadn't said anything about marriage. She'd thought her heart had healed in his arms, but a small crack reopened. "I'm sorry. I didn't mean—of course, I'll go without—"

He kissed her again, a soul-searching, body-possessing,

ever-after kind of kiss. When they came up for air, he asked dazedly, "Where were we?"

"I—I was agreeing to go with you."

"You're not going anywhere."

"Jason—"

"And neither am I."

She stared up at him and then shoved against his chest. He refused to let her go.

"No, Jason."

He frowned at her. "No, what?"

"I won't let you do that."

"Do what?"

"Give up your dreams for me. If you want me, I'll come with you. I know how fragile, how precious life is. I don't want to live it without you. But I won't tie you down either."

"Not even if I beg?" he whispered, nibbling at her neck.

"Jason, you're not making sense."

"Yes, I am. The only exciting part of my days the last few weeks was when Mom mentioned you in her letters. Or when I dreamed of you. The rest of the time was hell."

Hope swelled in her heart. She touched his cheek again. "You mean it? You want to live here? Will you take over the paper again?"

"If Dad hasn't hired anyone else. Okay with you?"

"Oh, yes! Yes! I've been so lonely." She threw herself against him with abandon, raining kisses over his face.

Instead of appreciating her caresses, he frowned again. "That's the only thing, Deb."

"What?"

"I don't want you accepting my proposal—"

"What proposal?" she teased, her grin growing bigger all the time.

"The proposal I'm trying to make," he growled, pulling her against him just a little tighter. "But I don't want you to accept because you like being married, or—or because it's easier."

Deborah stared at him before breaking into laughter. "I can assure you, loving you has never been easy, Jason Bridges." Before he could respond, she placed a finger across his lips. "I loved Randall. But that doesn't stop me from loving you. Or being miserable the past six weeks. Or pleading with you to never leave me again."

Her voice trailed to a whisper and his lips met hers with his promise.

"Deb, I just heard—"

They broke apart as Leon Bridges slid into Deborah's office. He stared at them, still wrapped in each other's arms. "Well, I guess the rumor I heard is true. Someone called my office to ask when you got back, son. Welcome home." He reached out to his only son.

"Thanks, Dad," Jason replied with a grin, slipping one arm around his father's shoulders but never releasing Deborah. "Have you filled that editor position?"

Mr. Bridges beamed at him. "I guess I have now. Wait 'til I tell your mother. We're going to have a houseful of grandchildren!"

Deborah stared at Jason, searching for some sign of restlessness or unhappiness. Instead, he grinned at both her and his father.

"Maybe you'd better go call Mom now. I need a little more time to get some advice from Dear Deborah. Once she's helped me out with matters of the heart, we'll join you and Mom for dinner."

"Right," he agreed, grinning, patting Jason on the back. Turning to go, he stopped to say again, "I'm glad you're home, son."

"Me, too."

Before Jason could resume where he'd left off, Deborah asked, "You want children?"

"Yeah, if you do. How about it?"

"Oh, Jason," she agreed with a sigh, "I do love you."

"Then I guess your advice is I should propose at once?"

"Oh, yes."

"But what will we do the rest of the afternoon, waiting for dinner?" he teased, his lips trailing down her cheek deliciously near her lips.

"I think I have some advice you'll like," she whispered, drawing him closer.

"I'm sure you do, dear Deborah, and I intend to follow your advice absolutely."

And he did.